The light brightened and started to lift. There was this distant roaring sound like flames blowing in a strong and steady wind, and a rushing sense of motion. It was so strong that I panicked, thinking, *Oh, no, we've fallen off the roof!*

By squinching my eyelids down hard, I kept seeing only the brightness of our ring. I sort of inhaled light and pushed it out again in a silent shout from my heart, "Fear, get away!"

Then I was flying. We all were, skimming up into the night sky like a bright ring of Saturn thrown from a giant's hand. I felt us turning and glowing and shining, filled with light instead of breath, as we sped up a curve of longing that ran ahead of us into the night.

I will never breathe again, I thought, so I can be like this forever—bouyant and bright as a star slung through the dark.

Other Bantam Starfire Books you will enjoy

The Golden Thread

Suzy McKee Charnas

BANTAM BOOKS
NEW YORK • TORONTO • LONDON • SYDNEY • AUCKLAND

RL 6, ages 12 and up

THE GOLDEN THREAD

A Bantam Book
Bantam hardcover edition / June 1989
Bantam paperback edition / September 1990

The Starfire logo is a registered trademark of Bantam Books,
a division of Bantam Doubleday Dell Publishing Group, Inc.
Registered in U.S. Patent and Trademark Office and elsewhere.

ISBN 0-553-28553-X

Published simultaneously in the United States and Canada

Bantam Books are published by Bantam Books, a division of Bantam
Doubleday Dell Publishing Group, Inc. Its trademark, consisting of the
words "Bantam Books" and the portrayal of a rooster, is Registered
in U.S. Patent and Trademark Office and in other countries. Marca
Registrada. Bantam Books, 666 Fifth Avenue, New York, New York 10103.

PRINTED IN THE UNITED STATES OF AMERICA

RAD   0 9 8 7 6 5 4 3 2 1

This story is entirely fictitious and all of the people and events described are Fig Newtons of the author's imagination. No resemblance to anybody, living, dead, or somewhere in between, is intended.

For Fritz, who said, "Why not a book as *well* as a deed?"

Contents

1

The Hands of Wechsler

I got a phone call a little while before Christmas vacation: "Val? It's Joel. I have to see you."

"What?" I said. *"Joel?* Why?" This was ungracious of me, but I was surprised out of my normally faultless social grace. I hadn't heard from him since the one and only letter he'd written me right after he started at his new school in Boston. That was months ago, after we had shared an intense and unusual—well, a fantastic—experience with swords and sorcery in Central Park. I had missed him since then. Judging by his long silence, he hadn't missed me. So why call me now? "Are you here in New York?"

"No," he said, "but I'm coming in to stay with my parents for the Christmas break. I want to talk to you. Take you to lunch, okay?"

Lunch with an older guy! Of course Joel was a friend so in a way it didn't count, but so what? Besides, I was grateful for the diversion. I had some depressing stuff on my mind. This had not started out to be a great winter for me.

Maybe it wasn't so great for Joel, either. He sounded anxious, which made me anxious, too, and very curious.

When the day came, I sat alone in the lunchtime rush at a coffee shop on Columbus Avenue, snacking out of the little pickle tub on the table. I felt nostalgic. This was the place where Joel and I had had our first real conversation, so it was not only my neighborhood hangout but *our* place, sort of.

As the time ambled by, I became less and less good-tempered. I was about to take off, feeling awful over having been stood up, when Joel strode in from the windy street.

He looked even taller than I remembered—could he still be growing? His chestnut-colored hair was styled in an expensive-looking cut (you could have put whipped cream on that haircut and eaten it). He wore jeans, a parka, and boots. A striped woolen muffler was heaped casually around his neck to hide the mark his violin makes there, and of course to set off his profile.

It was a thrill to see him and I instantly forgave the long wait he'd put me through. I mean, this was *Joel*—we had fought real evil together, we had made and lost a great friend and foiled a horrendous monster. I suddenly felt the reality of that adventure (which recently had been getting lost in a tangle of school assignments and general troubles) as if it had happened last week.

"Hi, Joel," I said as he sat down across from me. "Still biting your nails, I see." I meant it affectionately, but words had been coming out of my mouth all wrong lately. Apparently I had just done it again.

He looked down his long nose at me. "You've been eating too much sugar. You've got a zit on your chin."

Instantly my chin felt on fire. I had visions of a huge headlight blooming there just in time for all the holiday

2

parties. Rudolph the Red-Chinned Reindeer, at your service for Christmas entertaining. Thank you, Joel, for that confidence-boosting observation.

Up close I noticed that despite the appearance of things, Joel himself did not look so great. His eyes were red-rimmed in dark sockets. And he was not only taller than I remembered, but thinner. Too thin. Skinny.

I felt a stab of worry, but I wasn't sure how to express it without having that turn out wrong, too. So I said casually, "How's music school? It's funny to see you without a violin."

"I'm on vacation, thank God," he said. "Music school is killing me. The competition is unbelievable."

"You're not thinking of quitting?" I said, astonished. Something *was* wrong. I mean this was Joel, who lived for music—like the rest of his family.

"And do what, computers?" he said, sliding down in his chair. He kept his hands stuffed in his parka pockets as if he were cold here in the steamy deli. "Or I could be an investment counselor, like my cousin Devin."

"So you're *not* thinking of quitting," I said.

"I'm not an idiot, you know," he said. "I was incredibly lucky, getting into a decent music school after goofing off for years. I'm in Leon Tchorkin's class, for one thing, and I've been working with some really first-rate players. Lisa Walker is studying there, did you know that? Oh, no, of course you wouldn't."

This probably wasn't meant as a put down, but it sure felt like one.

A waiter wandered over and took our orders. As soon as he was gone, Joel hunched close over the table and said very intensely, "I can do it, Val—catch up, come from behind and win. Except I might go crazy first."

Now he sounded like someone I could talk to. "They

3

shouldn't push you that hard," I began, but he shook his head impatiently.

"It's not that. It's worse, and it's got to *stop*. I can't sleep, I can't eat, I can't work—"

"You're in love," I said. I wondered what Lisa Walker looked like.

Joel gave me a weary look.

"Okay, you're not in love. So what is it?" I said, trying to make up for stupidity with sincere interest.

"God, I must be desperate," he said. "I forgot what a kid you are."

I was not delighted to be reminded that Joel was seventeen and attending a college for music students, while I was chasing fifteen and still in high school. "Joel," I said, "if you don't come out and *tell* me, you're going to drive *me* crazy and that'll make two of us."

"It's my hands," he said in a low voice. "I have these—these incidents—I sit down to practice and my hands seize up. I can't play. It's got me *crazed*."

"Oh, no," I said, trying not to stare at his hands, which looked perfectly fine to me. He was pulling his paper napkin apart very efficiently for a guy with crippled hands. But if I had wanted serious, this was it, all right. Heck, it was catastrophic! Poor Joel! "How long has this been going on?"

"A while," he said, looking quickly away from me.

"Have you seen a doctor about it?"

"No," he said. There was something fishy about the way he mumbled into his scarf and avoided my eyes.

"You're not, you know, flashing back to something, are you? I mean, you've never taken weird drugs?"

"No," he said. "It's nothing like that."

Why did he have that secretive look about him, as if there was something he wasn't telling me?

I clammed up, thinking about this, and also because my

4

feelings were hurt. Joel and I had worked magic together, real magic, with Paavo the wizard and my own sorceress grandmother. And that made Joel and me special, even if we had ended up in an argument about how it had all worked out. The real world was not exactly loaded with great sorcerers, magical family talents, and kids who were invited into enchanted battles.

So what did I have to do to get Joel to trust me enough to tell me all?

The food came. I concentrated on that. I am an absolute sucker for turkey and ham on rye with coleslaw on top.

Joel shoved two fat knockwurst around on his plate with his fork.

"I don't have *time* for this!" he burst out. "I take ear-training classes, where they play a piece through three times, and at the end of the three times you have to have written out the score and gotten it right—the notes, the time, the nuances, everything. I keep getting distracted just worrying about my hands. I lose whole bars of the music. It's like that in all my classes; I've even screwed up in English, for God's sake!

"And," he added dolefully, "I've had to quit my only fun thing, which is to get together with Lisa and some other people and play chamber music in our spare time. What if this—this *thing* happened while I was with them? What if they told somebody?"

Imagine going to music school and spending all your spare time playing more music—and calling it fun! Joel had found a whole bunch of fanatics just like himself. He should be completely happy.

He put his head in his hands. "What's going to happen when I have to play my jury at the end of the term?"

"What's that?" I said.

"It's like finals in any other subject," he said, "but about a million times worse—a kind of dry run for the major music

5

competitions later on. You play in front of a jury of your peers and they rate you. It's death. I don't know how I'm even going to be able to prepare for it, the way things are."

"So you're not quitting but you might flunk out?"

"I'm dead," he said, "if things go on like this!"

I couldn't stand the idea of Joel cracking up at that school. Catching up in his neglected music studies had become crucial to him because of our adventure together. For him to lose it all now—it wasn't fair. No wonder he was so frazzled!

"I think you should tell your teacher, or your parents, or someone about this before they find out on their own," I said.

"Oh, sure!" He threw his head back and looked me angrily in the eye. "And be sent to some hospital for a lot of stupid tests and miss weeks of class and practice? Who knows what kind of damage they might do, anyhow, x-raying and messing around? Hands are delicate, complicated structures, you know? Nothing doing. And I have told someone. You."

"Oh," I said, flattered but worried. "Listen, Joel, I'm really sorry, but what good does it do to tell me about this—your—"

"Spells?" Joel said bitterly. "Seizures? It better do some good, because I can't live like this!"

Then the explanation hit me: a brain tumor! God. Poor Joel. I couldn't see any lumps on his head, but with that haircut, who could tell? I swallowed the last bite of my sandwich, trying to think of something useful to say, but my mind was paralyzed.

"I keep thinking my only hope is to go talk about it with somebody who, well, someone who *knows* things. Like your Gran, Val."

My chin wobbled and I started to cry.

6

"Hey, Val, don't—I'm sorry, what did I say?" he stammered. "I didn't mean to—Val, what's the matter?"

After some frantic shifting around, he stuffed a wad of cloth into my hand.

"That part's clean," he said.

"Yagh." I gulped. "What about the other part?"

But I was impressed. How many boys do you know who even own a handkerchief, let alone carry one around to offer to a crying girl?

"What did I say?" he begged.

I told him that my Granny Gran was in the hospital. She'd had a stroke, and she'd been unconscious for almost two weeks. The doctors kept telling my mom and me that there wasn't much hope that she would recover. Mom was a walking basket case over it. So was I. Two weepy baskets together.

"Oh, God," Joel said. "I'm sorry. I didn't know."

"How would you know?" I said. "We haven't been exactly close since you went to Boston. You never even answered my letter."

"I meant to," he said. "Honestly. I kept it. Look, I have it here."

He dug an envelope out of an inside pocket and handed it to me. Inside were the pages of notebook paper that I had used to write down some things about our shared adventure that he hadn't known about at the time, things that had happened to me when Joel had been held prisoner by the enemy.

Sorcery had swept me up again since then, in an adventure that Joel didn't know about at all. I felt a lot older than I'd been when we had first met less than a year ago. In magic, anyway, I was a lot more experienced than Joel was even if he was older.

I shook my head. "I never should have written any of

7

that stuff down. People don't know anything about magic. Anybody reading that would just think I was insane."

"Nobody's seen it but me," he said. "Nobody ever will."

There it was, on three-hole paper in blue ballpoint: how my little, slightly flaky grandmother was really a great enchantress who had been trained in an otherdimensional academy of magic called Sorcery Hall. Paavo Latvela, her old friend and wizard colleague, had come from there to fight a monster. I got involved in the struggle, dragging Joel in with me, because of my family talent for magic, descended to me through my Gran.

"You believed this when you read it?" I said. "About my Gran being an enchantress?"

Joel clutched his hands together on the table in front of him and stared at them. "I don't know," he said somberly. "Meeting Paavo, working with him—that pretty well wiped out my natural skepticism. He was a musician, and I've always felt that music is magic anyway, you know? But I've never even met your Gran. Maybe I couldn't believe she was special that way until I needed to. And I need to now."

"Except you're telling me it won't do me any good one way or the other, aren't you?" He blinked as if he was close to tears, out of sheer frustration and disappointment, I guess. "You're saying it's too late. Are you sure, Val?"

"I think so," I said. "I think she's dying." I felt sick, saying those words out loud. I handed back the letter.

Joel tucked it away carefully. "I guess I thought—I never expected—" He shook his head in bewilderment.

"She's old," I said.

"But she's—well, you know." He added furtively, *"Special."*

"Sssh," I said, looking around to see if anyone was near enough to overhear us. My Gran's magic powers were secret. "I think the stroke finished everything. She's out of it, Joel. She just lies there." Why had he brought this up and made

8

me feel so terrible? "Anyway, she's not a doctor any more than I am. What did you want her to do for you?"

"I don't know," he said unhappily. "Tell me what to do, I guess. Or maybe fix it, somehow." He looked at me intently. "Val, if she dies, what happens then? I mean, what about your family talent? Will you still have magic of your own?"

I shrugged helplessly. "I don't know, I can't even ask Gran. I mean, I could ask, but she can't answer! And what if I did still have the family gift? I wouldn't dare use it, not without somebody to teach me more about it first. And if Gran dies, who'll do that?"

"I don't understand," he said. "If she's got all this power, how can this happen to her? She can't just—just die, like any ordinary old lady!"

Which was something I had been asking myself a lot. Now that Joel had asked, the answer—or some kind of answer—jumped right into my unwilling mind.

"Magic doesn't make you immortal," I said. "We both know that."

We sat thinking about Paavo Latvela, our wizard friend. He had died grandly and bravely, as Gran had gently pointed out to me afterward. But he had sure died. I'd seen it happen.

And now Gran herself was teetering on the same edge.

I said, "Oh, I don't understand anything, and anyway, it's not *fair!*"

Joel patted my hand awkwardly. "I'm sorry," he said. "I shouldn't have come around asking for that kind of help. Forget it, okay? It's nice to see you, anyway."

My goodness, Joel was being charming.

He was also getting up to leave.

"What are you doing for New Year's?" I asked.

"My parents are having a big party, lots of musicians. What about you?"

"Going to a party," I said dismally, thinking about how, for the first time in years, Gran wasn't going to be part of a New Year's celebration at our house.

"Who with?" Joel said.

"Oh, friends."

He signaled for the check. "Listen, I'll call you, okay? Don't make any definite plans until I call you."

But he didn't.

2

The Comet Committee

My mom sympathized. "It's just as well, Valli," she said. "He's a high-strung boy, isn't he? These temperamental, artistic types are fascinating, but I know they can also be a lot of grief."

Mom, a divorced person who was turning herself into a literary agent, had dated several literary men who certainly qualified as high-strung and temperamental if anyone did.

"Don't worry, Mom," I said. "I know, too."

Not taking my hint to leave well enough alone, she pushed on with more of the same in the time-honored motherish manner: "I wish he'd come by and said hello, at least, before taking you to lunch. He's almost eighteen, isn't he? And living away from home. I'd rather you didn't see too much of him until you're a little older, Val. He might be, well, more advanced than you're ready for."

As we were both making lots of allowances for each other these days on account of Gran, this didn't turn into a fight, which was a good thing since it would have been for nothing. Joel didn't call.

So the day before New Year's Eve, like a jerk I called him, at his parents' place on the East Side.

"Seasons Greetings," I said.

"Hi, Val," he said. "How was your Christmas?"

"Fine," I said. "How's your telephone line? Have a nice New Year's Eve, okay? I'd invite you to join me, but my plans are already made." I hung up.

I put Joel out of my mind and got ready for New Year's Eve without him.

I was late heading out to a party at my friend Lennie's because of some chores that I was supposed to do, and Mom had gone all Iron Mother about them at the last minute. So I was not in a super mood to start with. And then I ran into this tall, thin person sitting in my lobby with his chin sunk in his striped woolen muffler.

I immediately wished I had put on my other good sweater, the one with a pretty yoke of embroidered flowers. But I sure was not going back upstairs to change. Not for Joel, who hadn't bothered to call me.

"Hullo," he said, getting up.

"Hello, yourself," I said. "Waiting for someone? What happened to your parents' party with all those musicians?"

"I'm sick of musicians," he muttered into his scarf.

He fell into step beside me without another word. In fact that was all the conversation we had until we got to Lennie's. Lennie wasn't there at the moment, though a lot of other people, guests of his parents, were. Lennie was, his father told us, out having pizza with some other kids from our school.

"This is Joel Wechsler," I said. From the look Mr. Anderson gave Joel, I foresaw some comment about Joel's famous cellist father or opera-singing mother or even his

12

conducting-prodigy kid brother. I could feel Joel, who was sensitive about all this, turning to stone next to me.

But Mr. Anderson said, "Not related to Abraham Wechsler at Harvard, are you?"

"He's my uncle," Joel said with surprise.

"Well, next time you see him tell him Hugh Anderson thought of him and Matty on New Year's Eve."

"Yes, sir, I will," Joel said. All of a sudden he looked young and shy.

"Go on back to Lennie's room, you two," Mr. Anderson said. "You don't want to spend the turn of the year standing on the doorstep!"

The Andersons' apartment was a favorite place of mine: floors lined with faded carpets, lots of tightly packed bookshelves, walls hung with rubbings of stone carvings from Thailand and Balinese shadow-puppets that look like exotic bugs in transparent nightgowns. Plunked down everywhere were futuristic white plastic chairs, glass tables, aluminum seats bolted to rods hanging from the ceiling—it was like a science-fiction sculpture garden crossed with a high-class Far East import emporium. You had to get used to it.

Joel did not have a getting-used-to-it expression on his face. I led him quickly through to Lennie's bedroom, which was small and cozy, its atmosphere of comfy clutter not much changed from when Lennie and I had played together here as little kids.

The tape deck was playing New Age music, Lennie's latest passion. The only light came from a brass incense burner on the floor, which made all his posters and photos of skin divers, coral reefs, and coasting sharks look very spooky. The scent of incense was mixed with smells of food. I spotted some miniature egg rolls on a greasy paper plate, plus two bowls of nuts and pretzels.

Joel looked over the tapes on Lennie's shelf. "Weird

taste, this guy has. Schumann, Reich, Hovannes, and Scarlatti? Plus all this New Age crud?"

"Joel," I said, "I don't think you should be going over Lennie's things."

"Music is *my* thing, remember?" he said. "At least they left some food behind. Want some?"

He held out one of the snack bowls.

I really was hungry. So there we were, standing very close together over a bowl of pretzels in the flickering light and the whispering music. I could hear every crinkle of Joel's clothing as he moved, and I caught a whiff of minty cologne.

"We don't need mistletoe, do we?" He grinned this wild grin and reached toward me. I remember thinking, Jeez, he is *irresistible*, and also, Is this what a heart attack feels like?

Then Mr. Anderson stuck his head in the doorway and said, "Valentine? I'm sorry, I forgot about you! Lennie's back, he and his friends went up on the roof. Why don't you go join them? But you kids be careful up there, all right?"

I gulped. "Sure. Thanks, Mr. Anderson."

Up there? What about down here?

Joel followed me to the roof. You could say that I fled up the stairs just to keep some distance between us. I felt him moving like a shock wave of warm air rolling after me.

A group of people stood on the cool, damp rooftop around a hibachi. By the glow of the charcoal briquettes I recognized a girl from school named Mimi, and Lennie's sister Tamsin, who I couldn't stand, and Peter Weiss from Lennie's science class. There was another girl in the shadows who looked vaguely familiar, but I couldn't place her offhand.

It was an odd group, but in a way that was the idea. This was supposed to be a sort of Better-Luck-Next-Year party. It was Lennie's idea: a party for people who had been having a rough time and who didn't really feel like whooping it up, because they just wanted things to get better.

Lennie, wide as a bear in an old tweed coat, turned with a smile from tending the fire in the hibachi. He was my oldest friend in the world and the first boy I had ever kissed. (That was in sixth grade, and it had been a real shock—people actually did that voluntarily?)

I had told Lennie a little about my magical adventures, but not much. He'd listened, he hadn't made fun of me or anything, but his caution had shut me up. I didn't want him to think I was becoming some kind of weirdo flake that he had nothing in common with anymore. I like Lennie a lot.

All of the Anderson kids were adopted from different places. Lennie had come from Colombia, but he didn't look at all like the sad, skinny kids in *Time* magazine photo stories about Latin America. He'd always been a chunky boy, solid and dark. He was shortish (which means not quite as tall as me, but I am a tall girl) with a heart-shaped face, brown eyes, and black hair that he kept cut short (it stuck up in cowlicks anyway). He spoke slowly, in this warm, husky voice, and often he stopped to think about things before he spoke. English was his second language.

People sometimes made the mistake of thinking that he was mentally slow, which he wasn't. They didn't hassle him, though. He was a competitive swimmer, and he was strong.

Which brings me back to the theme of the party. Lennie had been kept off his swimming team this term by an ear infection that wouldn't go away, so he hadn't wanted to go party with the other guys on the team. Just like I didn't particularly feel like standing around giggling and gossiping over the popcorn and stuff at Kim Larkin's big New Year's bash while my Gran was lying in the hospital.

Lennie was smiling now, but I could see the white cotton stuck in his ears.

It struck me, up there on the chilly roof, that I was really glad to be there, feeling sort of somber with Lennie on

15

New Year's instead of feeling miserable by myself in the middle of a lot of other people having a plain old traditional blast.

I also realized that I didn't know him as well as I used to. You know how sometimes you just sort of drift away from even good friends? I'd done a lot of drifting after my first magical outing, and more since Gran's stroke. I wondered what it would be like to have a real date with Lennie, by way of catching up with each other again. Maybe this party was a step in that direction.

At the moment, however, I seemed to have a date with Joel. He had gone to a different school when he'd lived in New York and he didn't know anybody from Jefferson, so I introduced him. Then we all stood there. I had this sinking feeling: It had been a mistake to bring Joel.

He said, "Jee-sus. It's cold up here."

"We came up because something moved us," Tamsin said. My teeth curled with disgust. Something was always "moving" Tamsin. "We brought some blankets, if you'd like one," she added.

Tamsin, a ballet freak, specialized in being the ethereal artiste with the intense gaze. Right now she was intensing at Joel, instead of observing that of course if you go up on a rooftop on Riverside Drive on New Year's Eve with nothing but a light jacket over your regular clothes, you are going to freeze.

Joel didn't seem to notice her. "Anything special to see from up here?" he said, looking over the parapet.

"We hoped to see the stars," Tamsin said, throwing back her black ponytail. She was from Korea, and she had long, glossy black hair that she was very vain about.

"Well, not really," Peter Weiss remarked. "You don't see stars when it's raining."

"It's stopped now," said the girl in the shadows.

Tamsin said, "We came up for stars. They'll come out for us."

If only there was some way to turn her *off*.

Joel turned his jacket collar up and leaned against the parapet. He's bored, I thought desperately. He thinks we're just a bunch of nerdy kids.

"It's all a matter of concentration," Tamsin said. She looked at Joel. "Do you meditate, or study yoga?"

"I'm a musician," Joel said, stuffing his hands in his pockets, his hands that wouldn't play anymore. I felt bad for him. "I study scores."

Peter said, "I don't think there are going to be any stars, Tamsin. Want some more diet Coke?" For Peter, this was actually regular human interaction. Being around Lennie sometimes had that effect on people. I wondered what Peter had to be sad about tonight. He'd won a prize at the Regional Science Fair, which had made him a kind of hero at school. But there must be something, or he'd be hanging out with some of his computer-mad friends from school.

Mimi Mustache—*Mimi*, I shouldn't use the name they teased her with in school—said glumly, "I hate to go back down, even if it is cold. I wanted to do something special this New Year's."

Word around school was that Mimi's mother was in some hospital, drying out, which must be pretty awful for her whole family. I thought of my Gran lying in her oxygen tent, and I got a lump in my throat. "Me, too," I said.

"We could launch our own star," Tamsin said. "Let's close our eyes and hold hands and think of people we care about. We could make a lot of golden light to send up into the night like a star, a star of love."

Nobody reacted at first. Personally, I was too embarrassed. Then Peter said, "You're not talking about some fancy

17

yoga posture, are you? I hurt my knee at soccer practice last week."

Tamsin said, "All we do is hold hands and think of light, Peter."

The girl in the shadows said uneasily, "Is that something you learned from your, uh, guru? Because I don't think we should do anything off-the-wall—you know, occult—without somebody who knows all about it. Is your teacher here, at your parents' party?"

Lennie said, "Tamsin's teacher couldn't renew his visa. He had to leave the country."

"Lennie!" Tamsin flared. "That's nobody else's business!"

"Come on, Tam, it's no reflection on you," Lennie said, sounding hurt.

Considering that he'd had his own problems lately with that ear infection, and considering some brothers and sisters I know, it was great that Lennie even noticed that Tamsin was having a hard time of her own. But that's Lennie for you: sweet. Though I guess Tamsin wasn't too thrilled with having her private sorrow spelled out to the world.

"So we'll try it without anybody's advice and see what happens," Peter said energetically. "An experiment, right? Come on, let's do it."

He grabbed my hand. I was too surprised to pull away. The girl I didn't know took Peter's other hand, and Lennie stepped between her and Tamsin, who turned to Joel.

"Sorry," Joel said curtly, "I'm just a fiddle player, I don't do magic."

He turned and left. We could hear his footsteps rattling quickly down the stairs from the roof.

I'd forgotten about his hands. No wonder he didn't want to touch anybody! I felt my face turning hot and red. God, why was I so clumsy and dumb around people? You'd think the grandchild of a great enchanter like Gran could manage not to keep stepping in it, socially.

"What's his problem?" Tamsin said, frowning. "We could have used another boy, to keep things more balanced. Oh, well."

Her bony paw closed very delicately on my hand, which felt funny—girls holding hands, especially me and Tamsin. She stood with her head back and her hair lifting dramatically in the wind.

"We'll make a New Year's comet," she announced, "falling into the sky from the world instead of the other way around. It's a present from us to the universe."

All we needed now was Walt Disney. Maybe Tamsin *was* Walt Disney, reincarnated. Too bad her guru wasn't around so we could ask him.

"You mean, like a shooting star?" Mimi said.

"A lucky star," Lennie said.

And the other girl murmured, "A wishing star." I wondered who she was and what she wished for to make the next year better, but it didn't seem like the right time to ask.

I didn't say anything because I felt foolish, but not as foolish as before, maybe because Joel wasn't there to sneer out loud at Tamsin's theatrics. *I* knew magic was real if anybody did! I should have been the one to suggest doing something on New Year's, though not something as soppy as Tamsin's comet.

Still, since the idea had come up, why not try? Maybe if I thought hard enough about Gran getting better, my share of the family talent would help make it really happen.

We stood around the glowing coals, holding hands. I shut my eyes, tried to think about golden light, and saw just darkness as usual behind my eyelids. I forced myself to think only about Gran. I gathered together everything I felt for her and just sort of beamed it at the sky. Words formed in my head like a chant, "This is for Gran. For Gran. For my Gran."

Standing there holding Peter Weiss's hand in my right hand and Tamsin's in my left, with the wet breeze pouring past me and the hibachi heating up the knees of my pants, I began to feel as if I really was glowing. Right through my closed eyelids I saw bright light spread on either side of me through my hands and everybody else's hands, making a circle.

The light brightened and started to lift. There was this distant roaring sound, like flame blowing in a strong and steady wind, and a rushing sense of motion. It was so strong that I panicked, thinking, Oh, no, we've fallen off the roof!

By squinching my eyelids down hard, I kept seeing only the brightness of our ring. I sort of inhaled light and pushed it out again in a silent shout from my heart, "Fear, get away!"

Then I was flying. We all were, skimming up into the night sky like a bright ring of Saturn thrown from a giant's hand. I felt us turning and glowing and shining, filled with light instead of breath, as we sped up a curve of longing that ran ahead of us into the night.

I will never breathe again, I thought, so I can be like this forever—buoyant and bright as a star slung through the dark.

Then a bolt of wild, blazing heat came zooming out of nowhere and slammed into us, splashing huge licks of light and darkness in all directions and exploding us away from each other too fast for sound.

My back banged into something hard that knocked the breath out of me. My eyes snapped open. I stood spread-eagled against the side of the elevator housing on Lennie's roof. All around there was yelling and tooting of horns and music blasting from parties and from people on the street below, making my head ring.

I saw Mimi and Peter hanging on to each other a few feet away from me, and Lennie in his big coat stomping on coals scattered from the upended hibachi. Tamsin crouched in a corner of the parapet, and the girl I didn't know was picking herself up off the puddled roof in a dazed sort of way.

"What happened?" Mimi gasped.

Still trying to catch my breath, I looked up. There was a fine, misty drizzle and the gloomy night sky. No star, no light-trail. No trace of an explosion.

Peter coughed. "Nothing, what could happen?" he said. "We lost our balance, that's all. You know how dizzy you can get standing around with your eyes closed."

He sounded very shaky, though.

Lennie kicked a glowing briquette into a puddle, where it sizzled out. He looked at me, his eyes huge. "Something happened, all right."

Tamsin uncoiled from her crouch and struck a pose. "Sure something happened!" she said. "I told you it would—we made a comet! We are the Comet Committee, and the New Year will be better because of us."

I was impressed—not by Tamsin, who didn't know what she was talking about, but by whatever it was we had done. But I didn't know what it was or what it meant, and I needed to get away by myself to think about it. I felt jumpy and strange.

I said, "Listen, I'm going to take off now. I'm pooped out."

Lennie said he would come down with me, but I just told him good night and happy new year and I ran on down the stairs. I avoided the Andersons' apartment so I wouldn't have Lennie's parents fussing about putting me in a cab. What I needed was to walk, to clear my head. It was only a few blocks, and after that weird energy flight and explosion I had just lived through, well, what could happen?

What happened was that somebody loomed at me right outside Lennie's building. Joel. Once past the initial heart-stopping effect, I yelled, "What are you doing lurking like that?"

"You think I was going to leave it to that bowelbrain to see you home safe on New Year's Eve?" he said. "I notice he's not down here with you."

"Bowelbrain!" I said. "Is that what they teach you in that music school—creative slander?"

This was not what I had intended to say, so I grabbed a breath and started over. "You should have stayed, Joel. Something incredible happened."

"What?" he said. "You made a star, right? You all held hands and chanted a mantra, and on the count of ten the cotton plugs popped out of Lennie's ears and took off into the stratosphere on their own, laughing maniacal little alien laughs?"

Well, that did it. Any idea I had had of telling Joel about the success—if that was what it had been—of the Comet Committee was wiped out by a surge of pure fury. So I just let him have it. Joel and I walked the few blocks to my house very fast, having a not very pleasant conversation.

"Joel, why are you acting like such a dork?"

"Your friends are the dorks. I'm just trying to rescue you from their babyish company."

"Lennie is not babyish!"

"Lennie is a jerk."

"Lennie is my oldest friend, almost."

"I hope your newer friends are a better class of people."

"You'll never know. I'll never let you near any friends of mine again, not after tonight."

"Oh, for God's sake, Val!" he stormed. "What do you expect? You don't belong on a rooftop on New Year's Eve with that bunch of flakes!"

"A fat lot you know! I don't belong with anybody, as a matter of fact, except wizards like Gran, who have something to teach me. So just shut *up*, Joel, or I'll walk the rest of the way home by myself, and if I get mugged it'll be your fault."

"Oh, sure, everything is my fault," Joel said.

"You embarrassed me," I said, "in front of my friends."

"Why should you be embarrassed?" he asked the night at large, making a full-scale drama right there on the street. "You behaved perfectly. I'm the one who messed up, right? I hope I haven't spoiled things between you and wonderful Lennie."

We stomped past three people strolling arm and arm and singing "Auld Lang Syne" softly together. Then we were at my building, thank goodness.

"Joel," I said, "don't come around here after months of nothing, and then not bother to phone me when you said you would, and *then* throw some kind of tantrum because I want to spend a little time with a real friend of mine on New Year's Eve!"

"Sor-ree," he said. "I sure was in the way there, wasn't I? And now you've missed your New Year's Eve kiss, you and your real friend."

He grabbed my arm and more or less banged our mouths together in a very angry thing meant as a kiss, I guess.

He said breathlessly, "Don't say I didn't try to make it up to you."

And he flung away, with his scarf ends whipping after him.

I thought, That's that, I'll never see him again; and I'll never get to tell him about what had happened with the

Comet Committee, either, which sure felt to me like magic starting up again. He would be left out, and it served him right.

And I couldn't tell if I was glad or miserable.

3

Leftover Hash

There was no sign of change in my Gran.

I had to force myself to visit the intensive care unit. I hated the quiet, I hated the strained, nervous people tiptoeing around with their flowers and their frightened eyes, and I hated the beds with the curtains drawn around them so you couldn't see but you could still hear.

I also hated that Gran had to lie naked under a sheet. I suppose that made it easier for the staff to take care of her, but my Gran was an old-fashioned, modest sort of person. That was how I thought of her, anyway.

I guess the only good thing about being out of it, with tubes taped up your nose and a transparent plastic tent over you, is that you don't know that you're laid out there like a package of steak at the meat counter.

Not that the people weren't nice. The nurses really seemed to know what they were doing, which was stuff I knew I could never do and keep my cool. I really admired them.

"Hi, Gran," I said, leaning close and talking quietly so as not to bother anybody else. I knew she couldn't hear me, but somehow it helped just to talk to her. "Listen, something really weird happened on New Year's, and it's got me sort of jangled up."

Jangled up and with nobody to talk to about it. I had broached the subject with Lennie twice since that night, but he just got quieter and quieter as I talked about it, meaning he was uncomfortable with the whole subject, so I stopped. And I was still too mad at Joel to try talking to him.

Barb, my best friend, who actually knew about my family gift from being involved in my last experience with it, wasn't around. She was visiting her aunt in Barbados for the holidays.

What *had* happened, anyway?

Something big, something full of fear and delight, and I couldn't figure it out at all. Maybe that girl I hadn't recognized at the party had been right, and we shouldn't have messed around with anything like that on our own.

If I'd been hoping for enlightenment from Gran, I was doomed to disappointment. When the nurse came around to do something with Gran's I.V., I left, carrying away with me the same anxious misery I came in with.

This anxiety about Gran was like a fog of numbness jabbed with hot, burning streaks of hurt and fear. It filled my mind when I couldn't find anything to distract me. And most distractions that worked didn't work for long. Even the Comet Committee mystery sank down into a dark place at the back of my mind.

On Monday I went back to school with everybody else, hoping the week ahead would provide some distractions. And there was Bosanka Lonat.

Funny name, right? She was no joke.

I talked with my friend Megan in homeroom while our teacher, Mrs. Corelli, tried to get enough order to introduce this new student. Megan indulged me while I gabbled nonsense about Michael Scott, the senior I was sort of in love with and who didn't know I existed.

Megan's span of attention was not exceptional. She interrupted me as usual: "Wow, look at that new kid! A real heartbreaker."

Mrs. Corelli was yodeling along about Bosanka—Bosanka? That was a name? She was a political refugee from Yugoslavia, and we should all extend to her the heartfelt hospitality and sympathy of free people. Mrs. Corelli was a sort of Rambo clone, except she had less bosom and she could talk. And talk and talk.

Bosanka stood up to face the class. We all stared at her with a kind of awestruck fascination. This girl was something else; something like an atomic tank.

She was square, with broad shoulders and hips, and blond hair chopped off shoulder-length like Prince Valiant's. She stood firmly on both feet, like a double-parked truck in a narrow street, looking slowly around the room while Mrs. Corelli reminded us all of the trials of the captive peoples of Eastern Europe.

Bosanka's eyes were pale as the Hudson in midwinter and not very big, in a moon face with high, rounded cheekbones. She had a mouth like a pinched-in flower bud, and she carried her wide chin high and thrust forward like the edge of a shield. No makeup, which made sense. You might as well put lipstick on Mount Rushmore.

She wore a pleated skirt, boots, and a baggy gray sweater with a high collar that didn't quite hide her neck. And that was some neck. Solid is a kindly word for it.

"Bosanka," Mrs. Corelli said, "would you like to say a

27

few words to your new classmates?" I'm sure she hoped for a stirring political statement.

Bosanka opened her pink lips and uttered two words: "Good morning." She had an accent.

"Jeez." Megan groaned softly. "Where's her tractor? Nobody could look like that and not be a Worker-Hero of the Socialist Republic of Something-or-Other!"

Bosanka didn't look like any kind of worker to me, though "heroic" was not so farfetched, as in "the statue was built on the heroic scale."

More words, four of them, followed: "Who is—Balentena March?"

Everybody looked at me, some grinning, some making sympathetic faces.

"I'm Valentine Marsh," I said. Why was I nervous? Because this strange person had gotten hold of my name, for some reason.

What reason?

Bosanka's mouth smiled. Her eyes did not crinkle up with good humor, however. They bored into me like twin ice picks. She said, "The assistant says you are my student host." She turned to Mrs. Corelli. "I sit with Balentena March."

I had completely forgotten about signing up for the Foreign Guest program (something I'd done in a moment of lunacy after Gran's stroke).

"Of course you'll sit with Valentine, Bosanka," Mrs. Corelli said. "Megan, you come up here and take this empty chair."

"Oh, no," Megan said under her breath. Out loud she said, "Couldn't we all move down one, starting with Jennifer?"

Jennifer Tieck, who sat on my other side and was one of the world's laziest living human beings, drawled, "I like it where I am."

Bosanka walked toward us. For a human tank, she was

quick on her feet. She was also menacing, a ridiculous idea but Megan felt it, too. Seeing Bosanka bearing down on us, she scooped up her stuff and took off.

The new girl plunked herself down next to me. She had no books, none of the load of paper and junk we all lugged around; no purse, even. No wonder she looked—well, entirely different from every other girl in the class. I was fizzing with curiosity about her.

She didn't say anything and she didn't look at me again. She surveyed the room while the usual morning stuff went by: Ruth Wasserman announced a planned demonstration against nuclear power; Margie Acton made a plea for articles for the next issue of the school paper. Margie had beat me out as editor this term, and she had no time for being friends anymore. Not with me, anyway. Nuts to her.

The bell rang and we all got up to go to first period classes. Bosanka was actually an inch or two shorter than I was, like most of the kids in my grade. I found this reassuring.

"Well, that's it for now," I said. "If we have the same lunch hour, I'll show you the ropes in the lunchroom and we'll sit together, okay? Meantime, let's see your program card. I'll point you in the right direction."

"I have the same program to you," she said.

"Are you sure? Let's see your card, we'll check it." How could she just walk in here from Yugoslavia and take the same courses I had, electives and all?

"The same," she said, with a shrug of her broad shoulders. "The assistant said it."

Which meant that I would have Bosanka next to me every minute of the day, that day and every day until the end of term. This was more than I had bargained for, and it started out as a very peculiar experience. Bosanka had nothing to say in any of our classes, and none of the teachers called on her, almost as if she were some kind of school inspector or visiting bigwig instead of just another student.

At lunch break she disappeared into the girls' room. I spotted my best friend Barb Wilson in the food line.

I instantly dismissed Bosanka Lonat from my head and finessed my way into the line behind Barb, eagerly turning over in my head the best way to tell her about the Comet Committee. She knew a lot about my workouts with the family talent, but we had not talked much about magic lately.

Barb had gotten passionately interested in becoming a prizewinning photojournalist, and these days she spent all her free time taking pictures or holed up in her makeshift darkroom at home.

I said, "Hey, Barb, come sit with me—I've got something to tell you!"

She gave me a cool look and said, "You got your special European guest to look after—where she at? I wouldn't dream of intruding."

Where she at? Barb only talked that way to me when she was fooling around or ticked off. She did not have an air of fooling around today. "Why not?" I said warily.

"Well, I guess you didn't notice, but why should you?" Barb said, giving me her dangerous, sleepy-eyed look.

"Okay," I said, "I'll bite. Didn't notice what?"

"Mean to say you didn't hear?" she said, in that singing drawl that meant she was *really* steamed. "She got her locker changed this morning. Out from between two black kee-ids and up to the third floor section in a corner that just happens to be all white."

"Oh, come on, Barb," I said, "how can you be sure that's the reason she moved?"

"Speaking of moving," said a kid behind me, "the rest of the line is up there at the meat loaf already."

We moved along, passing the meat loaf in our turn with decently averted eyes.

I said, "Look, if race was the reason Bosanka wanted to change lockers, school administration wouldn't have let her." I felt embarrassed and annoyed defending Bosanka. How could I be sure she wasn't a racist, anyway? What did I know about Yugoslavs? Maybe they were all cossack rednecks.

Barb said, "Who knows what she *tole* them for a reason? I can tell you what she *tole* Sandy Mason when Sandy accidentally bumped into her this morning at those mixed lockers, but I think it's too raw for you."

Oh, boy. Not that I was totally sympathetic. Sandy Mason was a bully who had taken my lunch money from me every day for a whole term of seventh grade.

"Look, Barb," I said, but she cut me off.

"Some other time," she said. "I like to be a little picky about my company at lunch. This food is bad enough."

And off she sailed. It looked as if Barb and I wouldn't be talking about magic or pictures or anything else for a while. I felt frustrated and teed off. There was no point in trying to tell *Bosanka* about being part of some amateur magic on New Year's that had attracted a response from somewhere— something that had pounced among us like a supergalactic wildcat, scattering us all over the roof, but something that had not been heard from since.

Bosanka, ever eager to please, arrived and cut into the line in front of me. We discussed the food, which seemed to be entirely unfamiliar to my foreign guest. She got spaghetti, garlic bread, Jell-O, and lemonade, and joined me at a table by the wall.

I tried to make conversation. I could have been more tactful, I admit, though frankly tact would have been lost on Bosanka. "How long are you staying?" I said.

She said calmly, "Until I find my people."

"Your people?" I said. "You mean your parents? Didn't they get out of Yugoslavia with you?"

She didn't answer, just chewed.

I tried again. "Aren't your folks here with you?"

She thought about that for a second. "Here," she said, "but not with. So, I have to find them."

The idea of Bosanka living in some kind of foster home arrangement and going to a new school full of new people speaking a new language made me more sympathetic. I kept trying. "I guess there are, uh, agencies to help?"

"No," she said. "Just you."

"What?" I said. "Wait a minute, Bosanka. What do you think a student host is supposed to do?"

"Want that?" she said, pointing.

I shook my head, and she took my dessert and finished it off without another word, from either of us. I didn't know what to say next. It was a relief when the bell rang: time for math, yagh. Somehow Bosanka vanished right after that class (if it had been me, I would have disappeared *before* math).

When classes were finally over, I decided to go see the assistant principal. Mrs. Denby was small and energetic and it was common knowledge that the whole school would fall apart without her. A lot of us (and, my mom said, a lot of the parents, too) thought she should be principal instead of Mr. Plastic-Man Rudd.

"So, Valentine," Mrs. Denby said, pushing papers aside and sitting back to look up at me, "how did your first day go with our new student? I gather she came as something of a surprise to you."

"Uh, yes," I said, not sure exactly how to proceed.

Mrs. Denby smiled. "I'd have alerted you first, but I assumed you knew she was coming. She did ask for you by name."

"She did? How did she know my name?"

"Why, I thought—isn't there some family connection, some mutual friend or relative?"

"I don't think so," I said. "I mean, not that I know of." There could be some link through my uncle Tim, maybe. *Very* maybe. Uncle Tim was not what you would call politically aware.

Mrs. Denby pulled a file out of one of the drawers behind her. "Well, she put your name down here, and she said that she knew you."

Could it be through one of Mom's authors?

"Valentine," Mrs. Denby said, "Bosanka has a very turbulent background. We understand that she comes from an old, aristocratic family that was broken and scattered by war and then nearly wiped out under the Communists. I don't know what she had to do to survive, but she's bound to seem a little—well, strange and secretive."

Not to mention racist, weird, and already cutting classes, or so it seemed at this point. I didn't know how to bring any of that up tactfully with Mrs. Denby. And besides, Barb might have the racist part all wrong. You can't just throw charges like that around.

I must have looked pretty dubious. Mrs. Denby leaned forward, coaxing. "Val, I don't want to stick you with someone you don't like, because of some bureaucratic error, but under the circumstances—if you think you can hang in there, at least until the end of this term—"

"Sure," I said.

Dimwit. Not Mrs. Denby; me.

Outside the school building, I found Lennie sitting on the stoop, drumming silently on his thighs, eyes shut. I parked myself next to him.

He quit drumming. "So how's the new girl?"

"I don't know, Lennie," I said. "There's something weird about her."

"Not weird, just foreign, I bet," he said after a minute. He knew what he was talking about. I felt a surge of warmth for him—I had been his first friend in America, years ago. "She's probably an okay girl when you get to know her."

Peter Weiss walked up and horned right in: "Call that a girl? Bosanka-the-tanka!"

Lennie said amiably, "So what are you, Peter-the-parking-meter?"

"She's weird," Peter said, making me wish instantly that I had picked another word to describe her myself. "Jason Scales tried to talk to her, and she gave him this fish-eyed look you wouldn't believe. But she talks to Val. Only to Val, in fact, from what I hear. Hey, Val, maybe she's queer, and she's stuck on you!"

"Peter, you're a pig," I said.

Predictably, he oinked at me. Peter was a bright jerk, what a country neighbor of Uncle Tim's once described as a "studious idiot." Whatever had happened on New Year's, it hadn't changed him a bit. Too bad.

"So where's old Coffee Grounds from?" he went on. This was a typical Peter connection: Bosanka = Sanka = Coffee Grounds. You would never have guessed that Peter was a candidate for a National Science Scholarship—if nobody killed him first.

"Yugoslavia, according to Corelli," I said.

"Yeah?" Peter said, interested. "So where's she now? Off changing her armor or something?"

"I don't know," I said. "She doesn't live with me, Peter, she's only my foreign guest at school."

Peter said confidentially, "Well, she doesn't come from Yugoslavia."

"How do you know?" Lennie and I said together.

"The name she wrote on her attendance card is 'Bosanka

Lonat,' and that's not a name," Peter explained loftily. "Not for a person, anyway."

"No?" I prompted. "Then for what?"

"In Yugoslav restaurants," Peter said, "they have something on the menu called *bosanski lonat,* meaning 'local hash, stewed leftovers.' So 'Bosanka Lonat' has got to be a code name. She's a commie spy."

Peter, who knew a lot of odd things from living abroad with his parents on army bases, was obviously about to start in on his favorite subject. His politics were to the right of Corelli's, which was saying something. Luckily Lennie, in a rare quick move, cut him off.

"Hey, Val," Lennie said, "come on over to Tower Records with us."

I made a face. "I can't. I told Bosanka I'd shop for blue jeans with her."

"Blue jeans!" Peter crowed. "All commies love real American blue jeans!"

"If she was a communist, why didn't she stay in Yugoslavia?" Lennie asked reasonably.

"She's a spy, I told you," Peter said.

"Peter, go away," I said.

Lennie winked at me and stood up. "Is this ruffian bothering you, miss?" He grabbed the back of Peter's jacket. "Come on, punk, into the paddy wagon with you!"

And he hustled Peter, who yelled and lunged around in protest, away down the street.

Just in time. Here came Bosanka, walking straight toward me.

4

Royal Blue Jeans

"Where were you?" I said. "I didn't see you in our last two classes this afternoon."

"I go to the park," she said casually. "I study there. Good parkland, but the foresters make too open."

Foresters? What was this, somebody's operetta, *The Gypsy Princess*? "Too open for what?"

"It's no undergrowth," she said. "No cover for the game."

"Listen," I said, "the kind of games that get played in that park, you don't want any more 'cover' than necessary. Games like hide-and-mug, you know?"

She looked thoughtful. "I saw animals fenced in. You're afraid of them?"

"Don't you have zoos where you come from? The animals are locked up to protect them from the people." She gave me an unreadable look, and I added, "That's only partly a joke."

She still wasn't carrying any books. Obviously she didn't

worry about homework. My mom always said that kids from European schools were way ahead of American kids in most subjects. This was not going to make Bosanka popular in school. Somehow I didn't think she'd mind a bit.

"There's a store down Lexington, this way," I said. "They have nice jeans. Sometimes a regular human person can even afford them. So what kind of school did you go to in Yugoslavia?"

"No school," she said.

Aha. I remembered Mrs. Denby's remarks about an old, aristocratic family. "You mean you had private tutors?"

"Like that."

I whistled. "Wow. Your family must have been pretty rich."

"We ruled," she said, striding along next to me and easily keeping up. "How far?"

"A c-couple of blocks," I stammered. Could this be for real? "We ruled" didn't mean Daddy was president or prime minister or whatever. Presidents and prime ministers govern. Only one kind of person rules: a king or a queen. Bosanka the foreign student was claiming to be royalty!

No wonder she was using a false name that meant leftover hash! Nobody would ever guess a royal identity from that name. Besides, maybe sometimes she *felt* like leftover hash, being in exile and everything.

Or she could be pulling my leg. Off.

"You mean," I said, as offhand as I could manage, "that your family used to be the royal family of your country?"

She made an impatient sound and said, "I am highborn, yes."

I walked along trying to think and keep my jaw from dropping at the same time. I hadn't even known there was a royal family of Yugoslavia, though of course there had to have been something before the Second World War. You wouldn't expect a democracy—nobody had that then except us and the English, did they? God, if only we studied some decent history in school, and recognized the existence of the rest of the world instead of just the United States!

"Oh, here we are," I said. "This is the place."

We went into the store. A salesclerk hurried up to us. "Yes, girls?"

"We'd like to see some blue jeans, for my friend, here," I said.

My friend? Was that what Bosanka was?

"What size?" said the lady.

Bosanka shrugged. "Measure," she said.

Instead of getting snooty with us, the salesclerk grabbed a tape measure and got down on her knees to measure without a word of protest. And this was the East Side, mind you.

"My clothes got always made on me," Bosanka observed idly.

All I could think was, cloth-of-gold. I was dazed.

"Size sixteen. Over here, please," the woman murmured. "I can show you—"

"We'll look for ourselves, thanks," I said, anxious to pump Bosanka for more information in private.

"Does anybody know about you?" I whispered as we checked over the shelves. Mrs. Denby sure hadn't seemed to. "The FBI, the State Department?"

"No."

"But shouldn't they be protecting you?"

"I protect myself," Bosanka said. She tossed aside a pair of jeans. "Bad sewing. You should close it down."

Close down what, Taiwan?

"Look, what am I supposed to call you?" I said. What did a highborn rate in Yugoslavia, or out of it? Something as rational as "Highness"?

"I told you," she said flatly. "Bosanka."

"Bosanka," I said, disappointed but warming up again as I went on, "so where's the rest of your family, the, uh, the king and so on?"

She shot me a sharp look and I thought, Big mouth, what if the communists killed them all, like the Romanovs? I knew about that from one of my favorite old movies, *Anastasia,* about the lone survivor (or else an imposter) of the massacre of the Russian royal family.

Bosanka turned away again, flipping through a pile of pants. "That we find out," she said curtly.

They must be in hiding then, and she had lost contact with them. A lost princess! And I was her student host, out shopping with her for her first pair of jeans! Who knew what kind of bond could grow out of this?

Not that I was an aristocrat myself, of course, but I was some kind of special person, wasn't I? I had the family talent! Wait till we got to be good friends and I let her in on that! Even a royal type would be impressed, wouldn't she?

I saw myself in nonchalant attendance at a royal wedding (though I couldn't imagine a groom for Bosanka, exactly), at state dinners with tables as long as subway cars, on the royal yacht. The West Side wouldn't be able to hold me anymore!

"So who are you here with?" I asked, thinking of secret guardians, loyal retainers, giant faithful dogs.

"With you, Balentena," she said. "Which you know it well."

Another meaningful stare, but meaning what, exactly? Besides that, she seemed to be deliberately misunderstanding what I said. On the other hand, why should she trust me enough to give me straight answers so soon? I could at least show her that I understood that her position was serious and that she had a right to be cautious.

"You must be pretty nervous, being on your own like this," I said. "I mean, people must be looking for you, like agents from the Yugoslav government. How can they relax while the royal family is running around loose? Suppose the Yugoslav people asked you to come back and help them throw out the present government and—and restore the monarchy?"

She walked into the fitting booth, with me trailing after her feeling suddenly bowled over by doubts. I mean, how likely was any of this?

I didn't have the faintest idea how to go on. Lord or loon—which was I with in this little dressing room?

Bosanka swore under her breath in a language I didn't know as she worked her way into a pair of jeans that were too small for her whatever the size tag said. It was a little like shopping with Margie Acton in one of her fat phases.

Maybe Bosanka went around from school to school trying her royal fantasy-life in each one until they caught on and threw her out? So where did she really come from, Long Island? Not a chance.

"God, I'm starved," I said. Excitement has this effect on me. "Listen, I'm going to run out and get something to eat while you try on the rest of these. You want anything?"

She turned to look at her blue-denimed butt in the mirror. "I don't eat today."

"These jeans are made in Asia, where people are little," I pointed out quickly. "They get the sizes wrong for us. You don't look bad, you don't need to starve yourself."

She gave me this contemptuous look, which is not easy to do when you are half wearing a pair of pants a size and a half too small for you. "Once a week, maybe twice, I take a day to not eat."

What was this, some special Yugoslav form of anorexia? "Why?"

"For strong will," she said. "One who rules others must rule first the self."

Now this was serious stuff. Food is not a trivial matter.

"What kind of ruler, exactly, Bosanka? Do you have a—a title?"

She turned back to the mirror, zipping up the last pair of jeans. It fit. Closely, but it fit. Turning to see herself from all angles, she said, "Oh, many. First Hunter, Keeper of the Wild, Breath of the Horn, others."

First Hunter? Breath of the Horn? Were there titles like that even in darkest Eastern Europe?

"You don't believe?" she said, spiking me with a chilly look. Royally gracious she certainly was not, but she was under a lot of pressure, right?

"I do, I believe you," I said quickly.

"You need to believe, Balentena. I am as I say."

She walked up front and tossed her jeans on the counter. The salesclerk rang up the price. Bosanka dug a crumpled wad of bills out of her skirt pocket. She had more than enough, singles mostly, and she pocketed her change without counting it.

While the salesclerk folded the jeans, I went to the door and looked outside, half expecting to spot a limousine full of beetle-browed Yugoslav spies waiting. There was nothing like that, of course, only a couple of ladies in running suits walking a pair of little, wrinkly dogs.

Behind me, Bosanka said sharply, "Look, Balentena. I want you looking."

So I looked.

The inside of the store went suddenly dim—or was it the inside of my head? The aisle down the center, with its beige carpeting, was a damp dirt path. The racks of sport clothes were green and rustling undergrowth that led my eye back into dark, damp forest depths.

Close by, something made soft, nervous sounds, a kind of churring that vibrated with an anxious undertone. Where the salesclerk had been stood an animal like a giant kangaroo, round-shouldered and covered with short yellow fur. It was fumbling around with something it held down with its paws under a little fall of water from a rocky outcrop. The air was thick with a wet chill and a smell of soaked earth and vegetation.

"My God," I said, but not a sound came out of me.

I heard water splashing on stone, and some start-and-stop rustling noises from back among the trees. The big animal nattered softly to itself as it worked with what it held under the water—a bunch of wide, flat leaves held together in a wad. They were purple.

"You see," Bosanka said.

At the sound of her voice, the kangaroo-clerk jerked its head up and blinked at us, plainly alarmed. Its open mouth showed uneven yellow teeth and a purplish tongue. The startled creature dropped the leaves and began shifting nervously from one foot to the other, rubbing its paws together in front of its stomach. I could see the gleam of its dark, delicate claws.

"Bosanka, stop it!" I gasped. I caught the doggy smell of the animal and saw the panic in its bright little eyes. She—it—began making fast clicking sounds and wrinkling its lips, showing more teeth.

"Easy, easy now!" I fumbled frantically behind me for the door handle.

There wasn't one. I reached through fog and touched the rough bark of a tree. I sensed steepness dropping away around us, as if we stood with this human-sized and agitated creature on a high crag inside a cloud.

"You see," Bosanka said again. There was a scornful twist to her mouth as she watched me sweat.

"I see, I see," I jabbered, stepping sideways along where the front wall of the store had been, away from the ex-clerk. "I believe you, honest!" My foot slipped on wet leaves. I tottered and flailed.

Bosanka did some quick, intricate moves with both hands, like making a cat's cradle without string.

The foggy air thickened into a white blanket which melted away in an instant. There was the store clerk, coughing and snuffling and poking around under the counter. I slumped against the heavy glass door of the shop, breathless with relief.

The clerk bobbed up again with a little wad of tissues clutched in her fist. "Oh, excuse me," she panted, looking wildly around the inside of the quiet store. "I don't know what's wrong with me today. Allergies, I think, even if it is still winter. Isn't it?"

"It's the damp," I agreed hastily, shaking fog droplets off the sleeve of my quilted coat. "It can really get to you."

"Oh, yes," she said. She flashed me a grateful, terrified smile. "Now, is there anything else I can do for you ladies?"

"No, thanks," I said. "Have a nice day."

I shoved the door open and staggered out into the bright winter afternoon. Behind me I heard the clerk saying, "Don't forget your package, miss."

Bosanka answered, "I don't forget. You forget."

I headed automatically for the park, for my own landscape. This wasn't just a case of exiled royalty anymore. This was magic, and my heart was pounding. When Bosanka caught up to me, I exploded. "What did you turn that poor woman into?"

"Was a leaf-taker," Bosanka said shortly. "You could see for yourself."

"Listen, I don't know what I saw," I said. "Are those things dangerous?"

43

"No danger when the Keeper of the Wild is with you," she said coolly. But I remembered that she hadn't turned her back on the transformed clerk.

While I had the nerve, I asked her straight out, "Bosanka, why did you do that?"

"So you stop talk about Yugoslavia," Bosanka said irritably. "I am not from there. The school knows only a story, a smoke. You know a little what I am now, and I know you. So comes time to stop playing little schoolgirl and do what I want."

My heart pumped ice water. "Which is what?"

"Use power to find my people for me," she said.

If this was reality, it wasn't any reality of *mine*. I said, "What power? You're the one with the power! Honestly, I don't know what you're talking about. Whatever you think I am, you've got the wrong person, okay? I'm an American teenager, ignorant and klutzy, barely literate and backward in every way, and I'm absolutely not the one you want."

She said, "You refuse?"

"Yes. No. I mean, I can't do whatever it is you mean by that, 'find your people,'" I gabbled, imagining myself suddenly sprouting a coat of yellow fur and a muzzle and the rest of it, with a corner of foggy forest to go with me, right here on a Manhattan sidewalk.

Family talent or no family talent, I was not the class of wizard that Bosanka was looking for, that was for sure. Next to her, I was no class at all, which I needed very badly to explain to her.

But she had her own ideas about this. "What I need, you can do," she said positively.

"I'd love to help," I said, "really. That's why I signed up to host a foreign guest. But what you're talking about—whatever you're talking about, Bosanka—I can tell you right now, it's way out of my league, you know? Beyond me. I'd only mess you up, and you'd end up sorry you ever asked. Look, I failed a French test last week, do you call that power?"

I hadn't actually failed, but it had been close.

"Oh, not you alone," she said, frowning. "But with your friends, there is enough."

"Enough what?" I said, glancing around. "What friends?"

"Enough power," she said. "Among all the ones with you, New Year's."

With me? New Year's? Taken completely by surprise, I said, "You mean at Lennie's party?"

"Comet Committee," she said, nodding once. "What else? Bring them tomorrow after class, in the science room."

She walked away.

If I had any doubts left about the reality of what had happened back in the jeans store, they were put to rest. Stuck on one side of the Denim Delight shopping bag she carried was a broad, wet, purple leaf.

5

Silver Wishes

They wouldn't let me see Gran.
The nurses said they had her on a different floor for tests,
and I would have to come back later. I couldn't even sit with
her and talk to myself in hopes that she would open her eyes
and answer me. I took a bus home, feeling wrecked.

Now I knew what had crashed into us all the night of
the Comet Committee. Our pouncing wildcat from psychic
space had been Bosanka Lonat, and now she was here. And
she had homed in on me.

Horrible possibilities kept flickering through my mind
like trailers for bad movies: what if Gran's "tests" did something to her and she got worse—ultimately worse—and what
if once Gran died, the family talent was gone from all of us?
What if I was going to be left facing Bosanka with nothing?

A little more of that kind of thinking, and I would go
insane. Gran would be ashamed of me if she could hear my
quivering thoughts.

Didn't she and Paavo teach me, didn't they *show* me, that you don't sit around shaking and moaning, but that you put one foot in front of the other and do whatever you can? Even if the chances are good that you can't actually do it at all, or that you can do it, but not walk away alive?

The bus lurched and a large person standing over me lurched, too, and demolished my left foot. So much for walking.

Besides, put one foot in front of the other and do what?

For starters, I had to relay Bosanka's demand to the members of the Comet Committee and make them believe it. Not easy, since I wasn't at all sure what she wanted beyond a meeting of the group.

And how in the world was I going to tell them about what had happened in the jeans store? I trudged home from the bus stop, with pauses for the errands on Mom's list, thinking about how Lennie and the others (especially Peter and Tamsin) were going to react to that one.

Should I even talk to them at all? *I* was the witch's grandchild, the one Bosanka had zeroed in on. Obviously it was my family talent that had made the Comet Committee into something more than just a party that night on Lennie's roof.

My family talent had drawn her, like lightning to a steel barn. I shuddered when I remembered that moment of impact, now that I had an idea of what—of *who* the intruder was. Without me, I was sure, none of this would be happening, but how could I convince them of that?

I mean, they might believe strange things about Bosanka. But to reveal that I, Val, had a personal history with magic would really be asking for it. I couldn't help wondering if because of that history I should be handling Bosanka on my own. But how? I didn't have a clue. I desperately needed to talk to somebody.

What about Barb? She had specifically asked me to include her in the next magical adventure that came my way. Only this present magic was about Bosanka, and Barb wasn't talking to me because she thought Bosanka was a racist.

To tell the truth, Barb and I had been having some problems anyway. "The Great Witch-Girl," she called me sometimes. She thought I was arrogant. Well, I didn't need any of that now. I was shaky enough as it was.

I could phone Joel, who at least would know what I was talking about. But he had walked out on the Comet Committee, and we had parted afterward on such a sour note. I had no business missing him.

Besides, he had troubles of his own—his hands, his whole future in music. It wouldn't be doing him a favor to complicate his life with Bosanka.

Mom was home, reading Manley's latest enormous spy thriller and dictating comments on it into her cassette recorder. She was also crying, on and off, and there was a box of tissues on the table next to the stack of manuscript pages, and a big paper shopping bag on the floor with lots of used tissues in it.

I didn't need to ask what was bothering her, of course. We were both pretty susceptible to tears since Gran's stroke.

She blew her nose hard and made pulling-yourself-together sounds (throat clearings, sniffs, and so on) while I fussed around with the front door lock, giving her time to come out of it.

"Val? Have you been at the hospital?" she said.

I said I had.

"You're a sweet kid, you know that?" she said. "For a ghastly teenager, that is. I'll go over tomorrow, it's my turn."

We did that, taking turns. It didn't require a lot of scheduling or discussion. When you live alone with your mom, there are some things that you can work out to run

48

pretty smoothly if you're both halfway reasonable people, which we were.

This does not mean that we never argued, fought, or generally hated each other. I was sweet-and-sour Val, depending on my moods, which lately seemed to change from one moment to the next. And Mom had her own attacks of the crazies.

I had done a neat essay about this in creative writing class the term before and had gotten an A on it, so I couldn't really complain. I figured that I was storing up material for best-sellers I would write later on. Mom had said once, "Wait until you're a writer yourself, you can write all about us and embarrass the hell out of your father." We both had a good time playing around with that idea. But sometimes I wondered nervously what she *really* expected from me and my writing, and did I want to be tied up in it?

We would probably never have to cross that bridge now. Leaf-takers, something told me, do not write books.

Mom said, "Stick a couple of frozen dinners in the oven, will you, Val? All the pots are in the sink, and I've got to finish reading this before I talk to Manley."   .

After dinner, I lay on my bed with my earphones on listening to Balinese gamelan music that Lennie had lent me, instead of making my usual evening phone call to Barb. After a while Mom looked in on me and insisted that I get into my bed instead of lying on it. She had a theory that visiting Gran sapped my energy (which it did), and that if I didn't get more rest I would get sick myself. I knew I could not afford that now.

Mom also laid a shopping list on me for tomorrow afternoon, when she had to be in her office to get calls on a book auction she was running for one of her authors. I was too feeble and confused to point out the inconsistency of worrying about my rest on the one hand and loading me with chores on the other.

Mom in love was not always Mom at her best. At the moment, Mom was definitely in love with Manley the author. Maybe that was what kept her from noticing that I was more or less expiring from exhaustion and extreme fear.

I crawled under the bedspread and forced myself through three chapters of my history text until my head felt like a boiled cauliflower. If there's one thing I've learned from experience, it's that when magical stuff gets into high gear, there are no time-outs. It also felt like a vote for my personal future to make an effort to avoid falling totally behind in my assignments. My future as a human being, that is, rather than whatever weird animal Bosanka might turn me into.

It was a long evening, without a call to Barb. When I couldn't stand struggling with any more history questions, I sewed up a hole in the sleeve of my Sir George Williams University sweatshirt that Mom had brought home for me from a publishing convention in Montreal. Then I went into the kitchen and washed dishes.

Mom and I had this ongoing wrangle about getting a dishwashing machine, and how it was wasteful for only two people living together but on the other hand it would lighten the chore load on both of us, mainly me. Tonight, I was happy to stand over the sink and let my mind wander while I soaped and scrubbed and rinsed.

It wasn't Barb or Joel or even Mom I needed, really. It was Paavo Latvela.

Paavo the wizard was growing dim in my memory, which made me feel sad and scared and disconnected from myself, too. Certainly from the self that had joined with Paavo, Joel, and Gran to fight a monster. And that had been one heck of a terrific Valentine Marsh. I missed her.

Now I was older and more scared.

Mom stuck her head into the kitchen and said, "Doing the dishes? Sweetie, I appreciate the impulse, but it's late. That stuff can wait until tomorrow, it's not going anywhere unless the roaches run away with it all."

I thought of roach-burglars skittering away with clanking pillowcases full of swag slung over their shoulders and I started to laugh, and next thing I knew I was bawling. I hated getting all soppy so suddenly, like a baby, but I didn't have as much emotional control these days even when I wasn't scared to pieces.

Mom came and patted my shoulder. "Okay, let's start again," she said. "Just tell me, first thing, are you, personally, physically all right?"

"Sure." I snuffled.

She pulled out one of the kitchen chairs and steered me into it, and then she sat down across from me with her elbows on the table, waiting. I would have to tell her something. My mom has no tolerance at all for the family talent, but she's good at waiting.

"I don't know if you want to hear this," I said.

"Whatever's got you this upset, I'd better hear it," she said. "I'll try not to blow up. Oh—my God, Val, it's not anything like what happened to that Stowers girl, is it? Because if it is, I probably *will* blow up."

It took me a second to realize she meant Beth Stowers from eleventh grade who had gotten pregnant and been sent off to stay with some relatives in Ohio.

Mom had this look of comical dismay. She knew me better than to really suspect me of anything so incredibly dumb. It was just on her mind because of course the parents must all be talking about Beth, too.

I said almost gaily, "Heck, Mom, it's nothing like that!"

"Better tell me what it is, then," she said.

It was all so homey and regular and comfy. I blurted

out, "Mom, you must remember something from growing up with Gran. I need to talk to somebody who *knows* something. I need some magic."

Mom's face went grim. "Oh, no, Val—not again! All right, come on, out with it—I want the whole story!"

So then I had to tell her all about Bosanka. Well, almost all. I left out the leaf-taker, in the spirit of self-preservation.

Mom jumped up and attacked the dirty dishes herself, flinging angry words at me over her shoulder. "I kept hoping," she said fiercely, "that it was over, finally, after the last time. Jesus. Give me a break!"

"You shouldn't have asked if you don't want to know," I said. It had been a mistake to say anything, of course; *that* hadn't changed. Would I ever learn?

"Of course I want to know!" said Mom. *Bam* went the pots and pans. "Thank God this time I'm not going to be kept in the dark until it's all over and the damage is done. Your grandmother should be ashamed of herself, luring you into danger again!"

"Gran?" I was outraged. "She has nothing to do with it! She's in intensive care, for cripe's sake!"

"These things only happen to you because of her," Mom insisted, slamming down a handful of silverware into the drainer. "None of your friends have—these *incidents* erupting into their lives, do they? You don't see Lennie Anderson getting mixed up with magical strangers all over the place! This stuff finds you because you're receptive, Valli. You attract it."

What could I say? My head echoed with the awful slam of Bosanka's attention crashing into our New Year's comet, attracted by my family gift.

"It's all because of Gran," Mom added. "She's dazzled you."

"I'm not dazzled," I objected.

"Yes, you are!" Mom said. "Everybody's always been dazzled by her, everybody but me! Her and her 'gift'!" She calmed down and tried reasonableness again. "Tell me, Valli, what good does it do Gran to be so special? She's in the hospital and she may never come out again. So what's the point?"

"I don't know," I said miserably.

"Do you know I had actually managed to forget the family curse?" she went on. "Until you brought it all back again last spring, with the statue and the monster and that street person with the fiddle you were careering all around the city with like some homeless urchin? Even then, at first I wasn't sure. It was like remembering a dream. Or a nightmare that comes back over and over, turning everything upside down!"

I said, "Magic doesn't go away just because it scares you. It's in our blood, Mom. And Paavo Latvela wasn't some street bum, either. How would you know, anyway? You never even met him." I shoved my chair back and stood up. "I'm going to my room. I don't want to have this stupid argument again."

"Stay there," she said through her teeth. "We're not arguing, we're having a discussion."

She turned around and stood trying to stare me into submission while she had me sitting down so I was shorter than she was for a change. "Valentine, you are a babe in the woods. You have no idea of what you're up against, do you? This—this girl, wherever she's from, is making demands you can't begin to understand, let alone meet. Whatever your Gran is, *you* are no supersorcerer!"

"I wish I were," I mourned.

"Well, you're not. What will this person do when she realizes you can't do what she wants? You think you're invulnerable? Valentine, this is not a jolly adventure, it is a perilous situation!"

As if I didn't know, after this afternoon! But one word about the leaf-taker and I would have total hysteria on my hands, and my own hysteria was all I could handle, thanks. I said, "I'm *okay*, Mom."

Mom dried her hands as if she were wringing the dish towel's neck. "I don't have a chance, do I? I've never had a chance. You're caught up in the romance of it. And even if you survive again somehow, every time this happens it makes you more of a misfit, a—a weirdo! Is that what you want?"

Not that again. I said, "You're always saying I should have the courage to do my own thing regardless of what other kids do. Or does that only go for my clothes, and my hair, and not smoking, and things, but not for something as basic as the family talent?"

"A lawyer," Mom said, "as well as a fearless magician." She hurled dry pots into the oven where we store them.

But all her protective fury was useless, pathetic even. I knew it, even if she didn't.

I started to blubber again. "I'm scared out of my wits, if you want to know. I didn't ask for this, but I'm stuck with it, and you won't even try to help me! Well, I don't need your help!"

"Nevertheless, you're going to get it," Mom said. "This Bosanka is a student in your school, right? I don't have to be a witch to handle that, just a grown-up—your mother, in fact, and a member in good standing of the Thomas Jefferson Parents' Association. I'm calling Mr. Rudd first thing in the morning. I'm going to get you out of the clutches of this crazy girl and have her investigated."

I was aghast. That was all I needed! What if Bosanka turned my mom into one of those leaf-taker things?

"I have to do something," Mom said, reading my expression. "Someone has to put a stop to this."

"Fine," I yelled, terrified. "Maybe you could really help, if you'd quit fighting the family talent and try using it for a change! Without it, well, good luck!"

I got up and ran to my room, put the Out Forever sign on the doorknob—Mom always respected that sign, it was one of the rules that kept life manageable between us—and made loud going-to-bed noises. I opened and shut the closet door, ran the water in my bathroom, and so on. Then I stood in the dark and listened.

In spite of what I'd said in anger, I couldn't risk my mom mixing into this with or without the family talent. Her rejection of our magic forced me into using it myself.

When things quieted down out there, meaning that Mom had retired to her bedroom with Manley's manuscript, I slipped out of the apartment. But first I took something out of the top drawer of my dresser, from under the scarves and socks.

I went to Riverside Park, in goose bumps all the way. Any New York park is dangerous even in daytime, let alone late at night. For the moment, though, all I saw was bundled-up people out walking their dogs or running themselves.

One thing Gran had taught me was how to make a wish and get what I wished for, a technique I reserved for emergencies. It's not the kind of thing you want to risk wearing out.

I ran down the steps to the metal railing along the bank of the river. It's not my favorite place. Dark rocks drop straight down from the edge of the path to the water. You sometimes see rats there in daylight. I thought I could hear them scuttling around down there now.

On the other hand, something's got to eat all the crud we fling around, and I needed the river, rats or no rats. This is what my grandmother had taught me years ago: "Make a wish by running water and seal it with silver."

In my pocket I had the first thing I'd ever bought for myself with baby-sitting money: a silver-plated mechanical pencil that was too precious ever to be taken to school where it might get lost or stolen. For running water I had the whole Hudson River, sliding along in overlapping coils with a soft seething sound.

On the way over I had worked out a wish that I figured was fair and not too likely to boomerang. The thing was to keep it modest and positive.

Like, Sorcery Hall, send help! If I couldn't turn to my Gran, maybe I could get some attention from the place where she had studied magic.

But I also needed protection against my mom's well-meant interference. Well, more like protection *for* her than from her. Last time I got into magical trouble, Mom was caught up in it, helpless and ignorant. I wasn't about to take a chance on that happening again. And I didn't think I could cover both of us at once.

I needed help with Bosanka, and Mom had to be protected. One out of two seemed reasonable to try for.

Watching the lights of the buildings on the Jersey side and the glowing night sky beyond, I tried to clear my mind completely. I clutched the silver pencil in my fist and shut my eyes. My wish came to me in rhyme, which had never happened before:

> "Sorcery Hall, Sorcery Hall,
> Granny Gran, wizards, and Paavo and all,
> Hear my petition of worry and need,
> Come if you can and come at speed!
> But if you can't come at my beck,
> At least keep my mother off my neck!"

Not exactly the tone I was after, but I think my sincerity came through. I repeated this three times, including Paavo's name even though he was dead, and threw the pencil out over the water. I saw a little flick of white spume out there, and something that might have been a big fish jumped and fell back in right where my pencil had landed.

When I got home, it was nearly midnight. I took a deep breath and walked right in, not trying to be especially quiet. I really hate sneaking around.

Mom came to the door of her bedroom and looked out at me with a puzzled expression. "Hey, sweetie, you look a little funny," she said in a concerned voice. "Is there anything you want to talk to me about?"

I knew which wish I'd gotten.

6

Tears by Joel

In the middle of the night the phone rang. I was too tired to talk to anybody, but suppose it was Barb and all was forgiven? I grabbed the receiver on the first ring. The fact that there was not a peep out of Mom's bedroom told me that my silver wish was operating nicely. She hadn't heard anything.

"Val?" said a familiar voice—not Barb's, but Joel's.

I stuffed my pillows behind me against the headboard and settled back. "Joel? Where are you?" I said.

"Boston."

"Wow," I said. I don't usually get long-distance telephone calls.

He said, "I'm sorry I was such a pain on New Year's."

Good grief, an apology! Did they give courses in basic human courtesy at that music school? I was too amazed to comment. He went on, "I was kind of rocked back by the news about your grandmother. Is there any change, by the way? About her, I mean?"

By the way, my foot. Joel wasn't calling because he wanted to talk to me, he was calling to see if by any chance Gran was well enough to help him with his hands.

"No," I said. Same old Joel, selfishly fixated on himself and his own concerns and probably secretly pining for his chamber-music partner, whatever her name was.

Well, I had something to tell him, something that would knock his socks off. I began by saying that I had this maybe-Yugoslav foreign student on my hands at school.

"Oh, boy," he cut in, "have they roped you into 'building international friendship'? Don't waste your time."

"Hey," I said, provoked, "what's wrong with international friendship?"

"What could be wrong?" he said ironically. "There's nothing to it, right? For God's sake, Val, don't you ever watch the news?"

Something sharp and biting in Joel's tone told me I'd better find out what was going on with him before pushing on any further with the tale of Bosanka. Maybe he hadn't just called to find out about Gran. Maybe something was up with him that I should know about.

"Don't tell me *you* watch the news," I said. "You don't have time, you have to practice."

Dead silence. Then he said, "I used to, yeah, that's right. Thanks for reminding me. I'm feeling so terrific because I did try to practice today."

I saw an image of Joel clutching the phone with dried-up little bird-claw hands.

"Not that it matters," he added. "I mean, who am I kidding? In the first place, there are lots of people who play better than I did even when I could play. In the second place, great music has nothing to do with the real world of

59

ozone depletion and nuclear meltdowns, which is why nobody writes anything remotely like a Beethoven quartet anymore. In the third—"

"Joel, it doesn't help to get all depressed."

"In the third place, pretty soon nobody will be here to listen to anybody play this or any kind of music. Either we'll all choke to death on our own poisons, or our mighty leaders will get into a real snit and somebody will push The Button. Boom. No applause."

I was really alarmed now. "Joel, is there anybody there with you right now? Are any of your friends around?"

"Nope." He chortled. "None of them can stand me when I get like this."

He sounded a bit blurred, actually. A suspicion struck me. "Have you been drinking?"

"Me? Well, maybe a little. I could be possibly maybe an eighth-note drunk. A sixteenth, even." A pause. "Maybe I'll go enlist in the Army. If I time it right, I might just make it into Central America somewhere, or desert warfare in Libya. Or Iran. Joel of Arabia."

"Don't be stupid," I said sharply.

"Well, why not?" he said. "If I can't even make the world a little better the only way I know how, with music, then so what if I turn around and make it worse? Maybe I could get into developing new techniques in germ warfare. That's a very promising field, I hear."

"Oh, Joel," I said, pretty much at a loss about how to handle this barrage of gloom or, for that matter, someone who was even an eighth-note drunk.

"Latest word is they're training dolphins to carry underwater explosives," he said. "Cetacean suicide squads."

"Nobody knows whether that's true or not," I said. "The Navy says it isn't."

He laughed, not nicely.

I held the phone a little away from me. "Listen, this is all too morbid for me."

"Val?" he said, ignoring what I'd said. "Are you listening? I'd try something, anything, if I thought it might change things, actually make them better. Wouldn't you?"

"Try something?" I said. "Such as?"

"I don't know, something! Positive thinking, Voodoo, dancing around Stonehenge smeared with butter in a hurricane! If you had something you thought might—might give you just a little edge on the awfulness of things, wouldn't you try to work with it even if it was risky?"

I sat up in bed, wide awake now. "Joel," I said, "have you done something crazy?"

"Me? What could I do?" he said. "You're the one with the magic. All I have is my dinky little musical talent. Can't change the world with that."

"My Gran has my family's magic," I said, "and she's probably dying. So will you cut it out, please? Quit feeling so almighty sorry for yourself!"

He said, "Oh. Right. Fine," and slammed the phone down.

Depressed people sometimes do drastic things. Megan knew a girl at another school who had drowned herself because of some bad test marks. I lay there in the dark frantically replaying the conversation in my head to see if Joel had actually said anything truly suicidal.

Should I talk to Mom? That seemed like an invasion of Joel's privacy. He had called me, not my mother or anybody else. Maybe I should try to call Joel's parents here in New York? Or his brother, the prodigy.

The phone rang again. I grabbed it.

He said, "Val? I'm sorry. My hands are bad tonight. My fingers feel as if they're going to turn around and grow back into my palms, like with leprosy."

"Joel," I said desperately, "cut it out! Or I'll call the Boston police and ask them to go make sure you don't stick your head into a plastic bag."

"Okay, okay," he said. "I shouldn't have called in the first place. I was just thinking about you and feeling stupid about New Year's. I didn't exactly cover myself with glory, did I? God, why do I do this stuff?"

Hugely relieved to hear him sounding human again, I said, "You mean like calling girls you know in New York and getting them all depressed with you?"

"I do it all the time," he said, with an evil chuckle. "I have hundreds of victims. There's a regular subscription service: Tears by Joel, Moans and Lamentations. Next time I call I'll read you some jokes and we'll have laughs instead, okay?"

I said, "Don't you know any jokes by heart?"

"I can't remember them," he said. "It'll have to be strictly a literary exercise. Meantime, don't let me take you down. Make friends with your foreign guest. Who knows, maybe some day she'll be in charge of pressing the red button and she'll remember how nice Valentine was to her in far-off America, and she'll refrain. Voilà, the world will be safe—for another five minutes. Now, I really am going to be eating Puss 'n' Boots for lunch if I don't get off this line."

"No, Joel," I said quickly, coming down with a thump. I needed to talk with somebody, and there was no one better qualified to hear about Bosanka than Joel. "I really do want to talk to you about something, no kidding. It's serious."

"Now who's in love?" he said lightly.

"Nobody," I said. "It's magic, Joel. And it's dangerous."

I began to tell Joel about Bosanka Lonat.

He didn't say a word, but when I finished the part about the leaf-taker in the jeans store, I heard a click at the other end of the line.

Joel had hung up on me.

7

N.U.T.

"This is the stupidest, craziest load of baloney I've ever heard," Peter Weiss said. "You're telling us old Coffee Grounds is some kind of magical royalty? Boy, what a load of bull! She puts out some weird vibes and you're dippy enough to fall for it, that's all."

Mimi giggled. "Why should she need anybody's help, if she can turn people into kangaroos?"

Peter said, "Where do you get off thinking we're going to fall for this fairy tale, Val? Are you going into partnership with this commie, Val and Bosanka, Bull, Inc.?"

I could tell he enjoyed giving me a hard time, Peter-style, while fooling around with a little screwdriver from his eyeglass-mending kit in the innards of what may have been a TV remote control unit.

We were sitting together in the chem lab, Lennie and Mimi and Peter and me, waiting for Bosanka. It wasn't the whole Comet Committee, since Tamsin didn't go to Jefferson, and Lennie said the other girl couldn't make it. Four out of six would have to do.

Four out of six, and two of them were jeering at me openly for the story I'd told them. Only Lennie was quiet, watching me with a brooding, slightly spacey expression— remembering, I was sure, what I'd told him about my last magical adventure while I was still recuperating from the aftereffects. I had been a little loose-mouthed about it all with him as well as with Barb.

If only he would keep his own mouth shut now about my family talent!

"Sure, it's baloney," I said to Peter. "And Bosanka's just another transfer student, right? So how come she's quit going to classes but nobody seems to notice? She wanders around Jefferson just as she pleases, and nobody says a thing."

"So what?" Peter said. "She's got special clout because her family defected, and Washington wants them to be happy. So she gets to do what she wants, and what she wants is weird because she's weird."

Mimi wrinkled her nose. "She wears the same clothes all the time, did you notice? I don't mean she's actually dirty or anything, but she's not exactly pristine, if you know what I mean. Sort of junior Earth Shoes." Whatever that meant. Mimi was an air-head.

"You can always tell foreigners by their clothes," Lennie said. Behind those warm brown eyes I could see he was thinking hard. "She just hasn't figured out how to fit in yet."

Mimi frowned. "But something is going on, actually. There're these thefts from the lockers, just in the past couple of days. *Since she came.*"

Theft was not exactly the major thing on my mind in connection with Bosanka.

"Well," I said cautiously, "the school has broken out in rashes of locker-riflings and missing money before, usually

64

because of Sandy Mason and her friends. On the other hand, Bosanka did pay for her jeans with a lot of small bills, and she had no wallet, just carried it all stuffed into her pocket. I don't think a person who would turn another person into an animal would be above a little light theft to keep herself in jeans and Jell-O."

Peter jeered, "The only person she's turned into an animal is you, Val—a donkey, get it? An ass! Well, don't expect us to go galloping after you."

"All I'm trying to do is warn you," I said. "This is something a little special, okay?"

"A little special!" Peter said. "Don't make me laugh. A spy, maybe. A commie spy pretending to be a defector, that I could believe. That's what I'm doing here—checking out her story."

"Oh, come on," I said. "Would a spy tell a story like this, about how our Comet Committee has supernatural powers she wants to use?"

Peter said, "Listen, I'll believe all this junk when I see her turn somebody into an animal right in front of my eyes, okay? Without that, forget it. And she better show up in the next five minutes to do it, too, or I'm taking off."

"Turn who into an animal?" Mimi asked nervously. "Are you volunteering, Peter? Hey, don't waste your breath. Actually, we all should be holding ours—this room stinks again. Couldn't Bosanka have picked someplace nicer to meet?"

It always smelled in the chem lab. Today's fragrance was hydrochloric acid.

Lennie said, thoughtfully, "How did she know about the Comet Committee at all?"

"Val told her, of course," Peter said, pausing to swear at something extra hard to reach inside the remote unit. "You probably don't remember, Val. You were just yakking, you know, trying to break through the Great Stone Face there, and you said a few things."

"I didn't," I said.

"You did," Peter said, with his usual charm. "You must have."

I said, "Peter, I know what I've said to her, and I never mentioned the Comet Committee. Why would I?"

Peter said loftily, "How should I know, I'm not a girl."

Bosanka walked in wearing her usual: soft boots, jeans, baggy sweater. No books, no purse, just Bosanka as always, with her broad, unreadable face.

Peter sang out, "Well, hi there, your royal majestic and magical highness. Are we supposed to bow or something?"

"Supposed to listen," Bosanka said. She faced us and did a slow sweep of the room, taking us in one by one. "And supposed to be here all together."

"We are," Mimi said. "So is something going to happen now, or what?"

Bosanka said, "There was more of you New Year's."

I said, "We got everybody we could. Lennie's sister goes to another school, so she couldn't come. And there's another girl, what's her name—?"

Lennie squirmed. "Uh, she's not around. I mean, she's gone out of town."

"And one more," Bosanka said. "Has to be seven. It was a boy, comes with you, Balentena."

"He does?" Peter said, looking up from his project to leer at me. "Who is this lucky guy?"

Lennie said, "Shut up, Peter. Joel isn't one of us."

"Yes, Jawl, he was there, New Year's," Bosanka said. How *did* she know that?

"Only by accident," Lennie objected. "He crashed our party and left early."

Bosanka said, "Not by accident, and he didn't go. He stayed, down in the street. He belongs."

I had a strong urge to protect Joel. "He doesn't even live here," I protested. "He's in Boston."

"Then bring him." Bosanka strafed us again with her eyes. "This is bad, only some of you here. Next time everybody better come. I only go through this once, now. So you tell the rest what I said."

Peter said, "Oh, talk's cheap, you know? We want a demonstration. So who are you going to turn into a critter, your royal thingamajig? Val says you do a nifty kangaroo."

Mimi giggled behind her hand. "Look out, Peter, you'll get her mad and she'll turn herself into a polar bear and chomp us up."

Lennie said gruffly, "Oh, come on, let's keep quiet for a minute and listen, how about that? I'd like to hear what Bosanka has to say."

Peter shrugged. Mimi sighed and looked out the window the way she did in most of her classes most of the time.

Bosanka started right in. "I don't come from here. Where I lived, my people are lords of everything. They hunt over the whole world, the land and the sea. Even in the skies, the Lords of the Air have their ways to catch flying quarry." Her eyelids fluttered and she looked nervous for a second. Then her expression closed down again and she went on.

"I was one of the Lords of the Heights, hunter of the high forests. Came time for me to go on my dream-hunt. A—a great animal guides me, not like you have here. Except maybe a tiger, a little." She sounded unsure, and it occurred to me that she was having some trouble with the details of her story.

She scowled. "It was treachery, some snare set for me. I went in a trap, a dark place, very dark and still. But I got out. When I come home, everyone is gone, gone a long time already. All of them, lords of every domain, and all the creatures, too. Nothing left."

She paused a minute, daring us to interrupt or make a wisecrack. Nobody did, though Mimi was humming audibly to herself to show how lightly she took all this.

I could hear kids playing ball outside against the wall in the school yard, and on the lab tabletop in front of me there was an old white stain in the shape of a shark. Reality did not fade away. But Bosanka brought her own reality with her: alienness, a hint of fog and distance.

There was an awful lot of reality stuffed into that smelly lab room just then. It felt heavy and crowded in there, and I wasn't surprised that Mimi hummed and Lennie looked strained and anxious. Only Peter seemed completely unaffected, fiddling with his silly machine as if nothing else was going on.

"So," Bosanka went on, "I look for them. I made my own dream-hunt, to follow my people's traces. A long time I followed, over very big spaces that can only be crossed with power and dreams. I was a long time alone in places where no one wants to be alone."

She stopped, her whole body cramped around hidden feelings. It was kind of awful. I had this urge to go and pat her on the shoulder or something, and I believed in the terribleness of the time she'd had right from the bottom of my heart. She reminded me of how I'd been feeling lately about my Gran.

Then she cocked her head, as if listening, with an expression of fierce concentration.

"One day, I hear something. A cry of power, a voice to cross any distance, a call from my people to me. I came to where it sounded, because right away the voice is still again, I don't hear it anymore. But now I am here, on your world. And I go searching. But though I search hard, I find nothing.

How can I find? Right from starting, this place makes me a headache. All noise, gray stone everyplace, machines shouting all over the air—no wonder your people have no powers.

"My people have great powers. They should be master in this foolish place! I call and call, but hearing no answer. I don't see them—this place hides them, hides me also from them I think—but they are here. I heard them that one time when I came here first. So I stay, and I listen, I watch."

She slitted her eyes. "And on New Year's, I see what I can use to find them. You made it, all of you in your 'committee,' and I see, I come, I fix to this power you made. You look surprise—well, I was also. Strange to find anybody here with power! I thought, never, must be a mistake.

"But it is as I say it: one by one, you are nothing, but together that one night, you make a sending of spirit-light—oh, a silly thing, a weak thing. In my home, any highborn child could do more. But for here, for you, it's big. Big enough. Lowborn and ignorant you are, like all your kind. But you can make light that will shine me to my people. They will see me, and come to me, so I join with my own."

She stopped talking.

In the quiet, Mimi laughed brightly. "I get it! This is some kind of story you're trying out on us, like for a performance or something!"

"No," Bosanka said. "I say only real things."

Lennie said slowly, "If you did all that—the tracking and everything—why would you need us?"

He was testing her, trying to catch her out logically and make this whole thing go away.

Bosanka studied him suspiciously. Finally she said, "My strength is less, and this place—I told you. My head is breaking from it all the time. But still I stay stronger than you. What you have, it's not much." She looked directly at me, with a cold, brooding look. "Enough, though, if you try."

This was worse, much worse, than anything I'd expected. I felt helpless, stupid, and scared.

Peter said loudly, "Well, what you have isn't so hot, either, you know? I've got better things to do than listen to this crud."

"I didn't finish," Bosanka snapped.

"Oh, right, sorry, your royalness," Peter said. "I didn't mean to break in, and I won't do it again, no indeed. Not with you being this royal person and all."

She snorted. "Who but a highborn could be here and live? Anyone less would run crazy in this place."

"It's not as bad as some schools," Mimi said.

"This place," Bosanka said, and she stomped her heel on the tile floor of the lab. "Earth."

Peter said, "So why stick around? I'd climb on my broomstick and take off, if I were you."

"Of course," she said contemptuously. "Where you go, it isn't any matter." She stomped on the floor again in sheer frustration. "It's very ridiculous! But, here I am. So, I play being stupid child like you, I play to find my people." She pointed, moving her finger from one of us to another. "And soon you bring them for me."

Mimi whispered to me, "I am not hearing this. I must have taken pills at lunch and forgotten about it, that's all. Or I'm flashing."

Lennie frowned. "I still don't understand exactly what you want us to do."

Bosanka fixed him with her pale gaze. "On New Year's, you used power, you and these others. This weekend you will make the committee and use power again, for me."

Peter began to clap his hands. "Great!" he said. "I've

always wondered what kind of science fiction they did over there in those commie countries."

Mimi said, "Oh, Peter, what's that science-fiction trash you read got to do with anything?"

Peter grinned. "Didn't you hear? Bosanka-the-tanka isn't just a foreigner. She thinks she's an *alien,* man! From this other world, where she was a lord of the whatnot, remember? She must be a real SF freak."

"Peter," I warned him. I tried to, anyway. "It's no joke."

"No, it's not funny enough," Peter said. "Jeez, Bosanka, the least you could do is get a pair of Mr. Spock ears. I mean, we're not exactly naive about this stuff in this country. SF has been around for a long time."

Bosanka pointed at the remote unit. "You fool with junk, these wires and cells, and you think this makes smart? What's funny is you."

Lennie shook his head, like he was shaking off all the argument and nonsense and trying to push through to the sense, if there was any. "Okay, but he's right, isn't he? You just told us that you come from another world, looking for these 'people.' "

" 'E.T. phone home,' " Peter said in a cartoon voice. "Only what we've got here isn't an E.T., it's an N.U.T."

Bosanka said, "*You* are the nut, junk-boy. This place makes you nuts. You have 'school' to waste your days, machines telling dumb stories of dumb people to make you dumb from watching! You think *I* would be born on this silly, baby world?"

"Hey, watch it," Peter said, coming up with a Bogart voice I never knew he could do. "You may be a princess at home, kid, but around here, you're just a tenth grader, got it?"

Mimi rolled her eyes. "But aliens have claws, or scales, or wings or something, don't they? And they're *dangerous.*"

"So's this one," Peter said. "Anything that can eat Jefferson cafeteria lasagna can eat you, too. And Val saw her turn some salesclerk into a kangaroo, only not permanently, so we can't go and check, right? I think I'll take off while I'm still human, just in case."

He pocketed the TV remote and started pulling his stuff together.

Bosanka said, "I don't dismiss you, junk-boy."

Peter laughed. "Ooh, gosh, I forgot—I can't leave without permission from her royal nuttiness, can I?" His face was red. He was mad. He started to walk out.

"Peter, don't!" I said.

Bosanka whipped some pebbles out of her pocket and clicked them together in a quick, odd rhythm. My sight went blurry, then cleared. The air tingled, like right before a thunderstorm.

Mimi looked around blankly. "Where's Peter?"

"Peter left," Bosanka said with a cold little smile.

Lennie didn't say anything. He looked sick.

I felt terrified and reckless. I croaked, "Bosanka, what did you do?"

"Maybe made him invisible?" Mimi trilled. She acted totally stoned, but the way I heard it, she had only dipped into drugs years ago and had quit real fast so she was doing it all on imagination now. She just didn't know how else to handle this.

I didn't either, but I had to try.

I said, "I don't know what you did, Bosanka, but you've got to understand: it's no use threatening us and—and punishing us. We truly don't know how to do anything for you. You might as well bring Peter back."

The little stones were gone. Had I really seen them and heard them rattle? Bosanka didn't look like a mighty witch. She looked tired and annoyed.

"He wants to go, he went," she said shortly. "He comes back in time. On the weekend when your moon comes full this committee meets again, *all* of you, to make the sending I want. Saturday night. Go and find the other ones, tell them, bring them. I am telling you."

The bell for the end of the period sounded. Everybody jumped except Bosanka, who strode out leaving the three of us staring at each other.

"Let's get out of here," I muttered, pushing by Lennie and hurrying past the sinks and counters with their swoop-necked faucets. We all pulled up sharply, bumping into each other just inside the door.

Something was moving in the hallway outside, lunging around and banging against the walls.

I eased the door open. A big animal bolted past. Foam flew and landed wetly on the back of my hand.

"It's only a deer," Mimi cried at my shoulder. "A cute brown deer, running around in the halls of Thomas Jefferson School."

We ran after the deer as it crashed and floundered down the staircase to the first floor. Another wild dash brought the animal to a clattering halt at the end of the hallway.

Its coat glowed in a patch of light from the panes of the big double doors to the outside. It was a long-legged, shaggy-chinned stag with short gray horns, terrified eyes, and a wet, black, quivering nose.

I whispered over the booming of my heart, "We've got to get it outside before it hurts itself in here."

"Easy," Lennie said softly, moving toward the frightened creature.

"But where did it come from?" Mimi gasped, squinting down the hall. She had a death grip on my arm, so I couldn't follow Lennie.

"From Bosanka," I said. "That's Peter."

73

And it could have been me. No wonder my mouth was dry and my knees shook.

Mimi let go of my arm and flattened herself against the wall with her mouth open wide and no sound coming out, which I guess was about as good as I could have hoped for.

I heard the soothing murmur of Lennie's voice. The deer, which stood about chest high to Lennie, lowered its head. If Peter was conscious in there, he must be half out of his mind with terror.

The stag pawed the tiles with one forehoof and tossed its head as if Lennie's body was already pinned on those horns. The eyes gleamed with mindless panic. The whole school building seemed to hold its breath around us, silent except for the grating sound of the creature's hoof on the floor and its trembling, snorting breath.

Lennie took another soft step.

The stag reared and flung itself backward. The double doors opened outward and spilled the scrambling animal down the steps onto the sidewalk. Lennie and I ran out after it, way too late. We watched the stag gallop down the avenue and veer westward, toward the park.

Lennie panted, "It's Peter, isn't it?"

"Got to be," I said.

8

Sorcerer's Apprentice

Mimi started to quake and groan. "I want to go home, I just want to be in my own room until I can come back *down*, okay?"

Lennie and I put her on an uptown bus. Then we headed for the park, after Peter.

Poor Peter. The woman in the jeans store had been turned into some animal from another world—Bosanka's world—for about half a minute. But Peter—that deer was of our own world. It looked like a change that could stick because it belonged here, it fit. I still had the dried slop from the deer's mouth on my hand.

Lennie walked alongside me. "Hey, Val. Say something."

"In a minute," I said.

"Well," he said, "then I will. I didn't really believe that stuff you told me last fall about messing around with magic and your Gran being a—a *bruja*, a witch, a good witch, and all. But I do now. I also believe we are in deep trouble."

We walked across the park toward the north side of the rowboat lake. Nobody was out there, of course; the lake was mostly iced over.

"It's all my fault." I groaned out loud. I felt a wave of dismal anger: I needed Gran's help, how could she leave me on my own like this?

There's a little wooden gazebo on the west shore of the lake. I stumped inside and sat down, hunching deep into my coat.

Lennie put his books down on the bench next to me and stood looking out at the ice on the lake. His body swayed to some inner beat. He probably didn't even see the sawhorses lined up crookedly about fifteen feet out on the ice, with cardboard signs in red lettering hung on them that said Danger plus a lot of smaller print. I wondered who had walked out on the ice to set them there, and how come whoever it was hadn't fallen through because of the Danger.

"It's my *fault*," I said again.

Lennie sighed patiently. "Come on," he said over his shoulder. "You didn't turn Peter into a deer, Bosanka did. I keep wanting not to believe it, but I saw those horns." He let out a whistle. "They were *sharp*. And where did that thing come from, if it wasn't Peter?"

I muttered miserably, "I never should have called the meeting. I thought everybody would just naturally listen to me and act sensible because I told them to, right? And look what happened! Suppose a taxi hits him? I mean, he's such a jerk as a person, imagine how he's going to be as a deer!"

To my horror tears began to run down my cheeks.

Lennie gave me a friendly bop on the shoulder. "Hey, come on. We'll work out something with the Brass Breastplate of Jefferson High. We'll be okay."

"You don't understand," I said. "The family talent has always been dangerous, but it was sort of—I don't know, an

76

adventure. Now it looks like my mom is right. It looks more like the family curse."

He flopped down on the bench opposite, legs sprawled out. "Listen, mothers get nervous. They can't help it, it's programmed into them by Nature, you know?"

"No, really," I said, calming down now and starting to think about what I was saying. "It's always been me and—well, somebody older, with magic of their own. Now it's just me, and other kids are involved, and I don't know what to do."

Lennie waggled his high-tops, frowning in concentration. After awhile he said, "Another kid was involved once. That first time you told me about: the monster in Castle Lake, and the fighting statue. Joel was part of that, was't he?"

"Yes. I didn't even know him then. It was because of Paavo that Joel and I met."

"Paavo," Lennie said, nodding. "The old street fiddler, only the fiddle was magical, and he was really a wizard from this Sorcery Hall, right? He needed you to help him with his magic because of your family talent, but what did Joel do?"

"Poor Joel, he was dying for Paavo to take him as a violin student," I said. "What Joel did was to get himself stuck in the subway as a prisoner of a monster we called the kraken." I sighed. "No, that's not fair. He tried to help when these three punks that were working with the kraken attacked us, up at Castle Lake. Joel kept the kraken from getting hold of the key that we needed. And then the kraken died, and Paavo died—"

There was no way to go past that fast enough. My eyes got all hot and swimmy. I snuffled into my coat collar until I got back in control. I mean, what was the good of having beaten the kraken and then having outwitted Brightner the necromancer and his wife Ushah, only to end up being run ragged by some crazy teen-witch from another world?

I added, "Then Joel went to school in Boston. End of story."

"Not if Bosanka wants him in."

I didn't have the heart to tell Lennie that I had already tried to involve Joel, or at least let him know what was going on, and the jerk had hung up on me. The prognosis, as the doctors kept saying about Gran, was not good.

Lennie reached under his jacket and scratched thoughtfully. One thing about him, he was always very casual about body things, which could be kind of embarrassing.

"What is it?" I snapped. "Have you got fleas?"

His eyebrows quirked in surprise. "Just an itch."

"Well, spare me, will you?" I said.

"Sorry," he said. He anchored both hands deep in his jacket pockets. "There's more, right?" he said after a minute. "*Without* Joel. The part about that guy who pretended to be our school psychologist for a little while—"

"Brightner, that pig!" God, how clearly all that came back to me now—the lush, juicy voice of the man, and his hound-dog smile!

Lennie cleared his throat delicately. "He came on to your mother, you said."

I poked him in the knee with my foot. "Lennie, he was after her, and me, *and* my Gran. Control of the family talent was what he really wanted. I wouldn't call that exactly flirting, you know?"

He blushed. "Me, either. But you beat him, right?"

"Me and my Gran," I said. "*We* beat him."

"Well, *we* will beat this thing, too. Us. The Comet Committee."

"What?" I yelped.

Some ducks in the puddles at the lake's edge flapped their wings and moved further away, to a less explosive neighborhood. Also less dirty. Right around the wooden

78

pavilion there was more litter and trash than anywhere else along the shoreline.

I went on pretty hotly, "Lennie, were you there just now? Did you hear what Mimi said? Did you see what happened to Peter? And Joel thinks the Comet Committee is a load of crap anyway, so why should he help?"

"Maybe it's better if he doesn't," Lennie said. "He's kind of snooty, isn't he? I mean, he's not too good at fitting in with people he doesn't know."

I frowned at the beat-up wooden floor of the gazebo. I didn't like to hear Lennie criticizing Joel. What did Lennie really know about him or about magic, anyway? It was Joel who had been a prisoner of the kraken, not Lennie, and it was Joel who had this mysterious malady that was driving him to drink, a little anyway, and cutting him off from me when I needed him most.

I said angrily, "Listen, I don't even know if I can persuade Joel to have anything to do with this."

"Just don't strain yourself," Lennie said mildly, "that's all I'm saying."

I sighed. "You've got a lot to learn about magic," I said. "As you said yourself, Bosanka wants him in, and she's calling the shots."

Lennie drew his eyebrows together into a dark bar over his eyes. He looked away from me, out at the gray ice of the lake. "I guess she is, isn't she? It feels funny, taking orders from a girl."

I snorted. "I don't like it any better than you do, but it has nothing to do with her being female. Bosanka just scares me to death."

"Want a Life Saver?" He held out a grubby roll of candies. I took the top one even though it was only grape flavor and had some pocket fuzz stuck to it. Lennie popped a green one into his mouth and put the roll away. "You know what scares *me*? That we did do something real that night on the roof or Bosanka wouldn't have noticed us."

"Right," I said.

"What I mean is, I guess you're used to thinking of yourself as, you know, talented this way," he said. "I'm not. It gives me the creeps. But I have to admit, I'd sort of been waiting for the other shoe to drop. Since New Year's. I felt something connect up with us, hard, on the roof that night. I just couldn't figure out what it might be. Now I know, and I wish I didn't."

I thought back to the falling sensation, the brightness, the interruption like a fist smashing our sending—Bosanka, homing in on what she saw as "power."

"Hey," I said, "do you think we *all* felt it—I mean, the comet or whatever it was we made, and then the shock when Bosanka glommed onto us like that? Mimi and Peter didn't seem to believe that anything had really happened."

"Mimi's naturally spaced most of the time," he said. "And Peter—well, anything he can't explain makes him angry, and we know where that got him. Yeah, I think we all felt it." He paused. Then he said, "And I think Bosanka's business is really with all of us, the whole committee, just like she says. So this isn't only your family curse, Val. Other people are involved, with gifts of their own—the whole committee."

"Baloney," I muttered. "Magic isn't just another human gene, you know."

"I'm not saying we all have magic, Val. But what happened on New Year's Eve—whatever energy we generated—happened because of what each of us felt, what each of us wished for. I'm sure of that."

I wasn't, but I did want to believe that it hadn't just been me, lobbing off a firework of my family talent all by myself, that had gotten all of us in the soup and Peter turned into a deer. So I didn't say anything.

"Listen," Lennie said, stretching out his arms along the rail of the gazebo. "Why did you bring us together to talk to Bosanka? You must have thought we had something to contribute to the situation, right? Or what did you think was going to happen?"

"I *thought*," I said, "that she'd take one look at the Comet Committee and realize that she had it all wrong, that we were just a bunch of high-school jerks and there wasn't a thing we could do for her. That's what I thought would happen."

In other words, I had been hoping that the total unmagicalness of the rest of them would camouflage me and deflect Bosanka from me along with them.

"Come on, Val," Lennie said, "come on, come *on*! We're for real, just like Bosanka says. The Comet Committee works." His eyes glowed with a wonder that would have been beautiful to see, except that what had caused it could also wreck us all.

"Lennie," I said, "I hate to bring you down to grubby old reality, but what good is a committee that's only half-together and a bunch of beginners at magic besides? And one of them's in Boston, and another one's a deer?"

He considered this for a moment, scratching vaguely at his neck until he remembered not to and put his hand down again quickly.

"I'm not sure," he admitted. "I'm just trying to point something out to you. I'm trying to point out that you're not alone in this. I think you're used to being, like, the only kid on the block, the sorcerer's apprentice. This time the sorcerer is Bosanka, and our side—our side is a team thing, or it's nothing."

Reluctantly I thought about this while I wiggled my toes inside my shoes to keep my circulation going.

Lennie knew me well enough to sense that it was time to ease off and leave me to think. He got up and leaned over the railing, looking down at the muddy margin of the lake. He bounced on the balls of his feet.

"Wow," he said, "no wonder no fish live in this lake. You know what's down there?"

And in his Lennie way he began reeling off a list of what he saw. "Paper, broken glass, peanut shells, two cigarette butts, some crunched tinfoil, two feathers, a white plastic fork with broken tines, a matchbook cover, some sticks, three mashed-up soda cans, and an evil-looking wad of black clothing."

I got up. "Thanks for the guided tour of the local dump. Come on, let's go. I'm freezing."

"Look," Lennie said as he swung around one of the corner posts, leaving the gazebo. He pointed at the outside wall.

Someone had drawn an animal on it, standing up on its hind legs and holding a blob in its front paws. The outline was drawn in a kind of dark grease, and it had the bold simplicity of a prehistoric wall-painting.

"Lipstick," Lennie said, touching the outline and rubbing his fingers together under his nose. "Phew, cheap stuff, smells like Log Cabin Syrup. Funny kind of graffiti."

"Let's get out of here," I said.

The picture was of a leaf-taker, and seeing it there, I understood where Bosanka was spending her spare time—in the most familiar territory she could find, our "parkland."

Which I knew from personal experience to be a center of power in its own right. If she hooked up her native magic with that, we were all going to be in absolutely unimaginable trouble.

Assuming she hadn't done it already.

9

Now Here's
My Plan

Gran had been moved to a private room. I had a few nightmare moments when I thought I wouldn't be able to find her. But I did, of course. I told her everything, even though nothing seemed to get through.

"She's a witch, Gran," I whispered. "and there's a whole lot of people at risk here. One of them's already under a bad spell. We can't handle this alone. You have to help me. Please wake up and tell me what's going on, tell me what to do!"

For a minute there, looking at my magic Gran laid out like a little withered-up mummy, I could have killed myself for having used my silver wish to protect my mom. What I *should* have done, of course, was to wish my Gran well again!

But could you make a silver wish for something like that? What if Gran was here for a reason I didn't know? She was magical, my Gran, so it must mean something that she was out of reach right now, of all times. In all this time visiting at the hospital it had never before occurred to me to try to think about this situation from her point of view.

Suppose she wasn't dying at all? Suppose she just had to have some rest time, uninterrupted by anything or anybody, so afterward she could live for a long time to come? Or suppose Sorcery Hall had called on her suddenly and she had left her body here while her powerful spirit went off to do something that nobody else could do?

Well, why didn't she warn me? Why hadn't she seen Bosanka coming and tipped me off, or left me with some kind of advice or special spell to deal with the girl-witch from her horrible planet of hunters?

Or maybe Gran had simply made a mistake. Maybe I had wasted my silver wish in spite of being gifted with the family talent; maybe Gran had made a wrong choice, too. The machines at the head of Gran's bed made sucking, sighing noises something like the noises I was making, crying, while my mind went on churning and churning.

If Gran did wake up, she'd probably say I was right to make a wish to safeguard my mom, who couldn't, after all, protect herself. Maybe Gran could protect herself, even lying in a coma. And I had to try to protect myself, which maybe I could even manage to do.

I had the family talent, after all, and I had some experience with magic. I didn't have access to Gran's wisdom, but I knew a thing or two—more than anybody else in the Comet Committee did.

In fact, they didn't know a thing. It hit me like a breaker, big and cold: no matter how much talent each of those kids might have—Lennie, Tamsin (yuk), dippy Mimi (really, could *she* have any magic?), Peter, Joel, and let's not forget the mystery girl I didn't know—no matter how much, it was pretty clear that none of them had as much experience as I had.

Compared to them, I had wisdom, the way Gran had wisdom compared to me.

But talent or no talent, experience or no experience, you could never know for sure why somebody else did what they did or how to help them if they had made a mistake. All you could be sure of was that usually people have good reasons for their actions, even if those reasons aren't obvious to anybody else.

I decided I had made the right wish, probably; and I kissed Gran on the forehead—her skin was very dry and cool—and went home.

That same Wednesday evening we met at Lennie's: Mimi, Tamsin, me, and Lennie, of course. His parents were at the theater, and his youngest sister was sleeping over at her friend's house.

I got there late, right from the hospital. Everybody gave me funny looks when I came in except Lennie. He was wiping down his favorite shoes, a pair of old, scuffed work boots, with an oily rag.

"What?" I said to the group at large. "What are you all staring at?"

Tamsin said, "Lennie says you're a witch."

"Lennie!" I roared.

He said, "People have to know, Val. Us in the committee, I mean."

"Who decided that?" I shot back. "It's my secret, remember? My *family* secret. You had no right—"

He stopped working on the shoes. "You don't go into a tough game with your team all shaking and wondering what they've got that's strong enough to stop the other guys."

The whales and giant groupers and things stared from the posters on the walls. Lennie was taking Mrs. Moorehouse's elective "Spaceship Earth," which was heavy on ecology. He was deeply into marine life-systems, which was not strange for a kid who had once loved to play at being Captain Nemo in his submarine headquarters, twenty thousand leagues under the sea, with me playing everybody else in the story.

That had been a long time ago, and we weren't playing now.

"I don't know if I can stop Bosanka," I admitted. "My Gran could, but she's sick. So we can't count on my family talent, which is why it was wrong to mention it, Lennie."

Mimi said quickly, "But your Gran *could* wake up, or you could figure out something magical yourself."

"Anything's possible, I guess," I said.

Tamsin said, "I don't believe any of it. Why should your family have magic? What's so special about you?"

I don't need this, I thought, I could just walk out of here. But I *did* need this. Or anyway, I needed the members of the Comet Committee. Maybe I was special, but Bosanka wanted them all.

I said, "I don't know how come, Tamsin. I think it has something to do with Gran being from Scotland. They have people there they say are 'fey,' with psychic talents and stuff."

"That's Ireland," Tamsin said.

Lennie said patiently, "They're all Celts, Tam."

I went on, "Whatever I have of the talent is just because I'm Gran's grandchild."

Mimi said, "What do your parents think about this?"

"My dad went to live in Alaska years ago," I said. "I don't think he knows anything about it. My mom knows. She hates the whole idea."

"I bet," Tamsin said shrewdly. "She'd deny any of this was true if we asked her, wouldn't she? She'd tell us you're just very imaginative."

"Probably," I said. "So don't bother asking her. Ask me. What would convince you, Tamsin?"

"How about a demonstration?"

Mimi yelled out, "NO! That's what Peter said, and Bosanka turned him into a deer."

Tamsin said, "Oh, for crying out loud!"

"Tammy, listen," Lennie insisted. "I was there, I saw what happened to Peter. I should have let him gore me a little so I'd have evidence to show you."

"But he didn't," Tamsin said, flopping down in the old red sling-chair by Lennie's window. "So there is no evidence, is there?"

I said, "There's only what happened."

"What you say happened," Tamsin said.

"What all three of us say happened."

She shrugged and started doing slow leg-stretches. She was wearing a big old shirt of Lennie's over a leotard, and purple leg-warmers—very picturesque.

Lennie turned to me. "I think you'd better tell the whole story, Val, your way. About your family, too."

So I sat on his bed and told about Paavo and the kraken and Joel and Dr. Brightner and Ushah the witch—and now, Bosanka.

Mimi wailed, "This is crazy! I'm going to tell my mother!"

"What could she do?" Lennie objected. "She could get hurt, Mimi."

"Well, we could, too," she whined. "What about us?"

"Look," I said, "if you tell your parents they'll just freak, they won't know what to do. As far as we know, there are no grown-ups around with a better handle on this situation than we have ourselves. At least I've had some, uh, experience with this kind of stuff."

" 'Experience,' " Tamsin jeered. "I bet this whole mess is all on account of you."

That was hitting close to home. I snapped back, "Who first suggested 'making a star' on the roof on New Year's?"

"Hey, come on," Lennie said wearily. "Passing the blame around won't get us anywhere. We've only got till Saturday to figure out what to do."

Tamsin tossed her long black hair. "*You've* got," she said. "I never said I was getting mixed up with some loony tune from outer space."

"You have to help!" Mimi cried. "Otherwise she'll turn us all into animals!"

Lennie said, "Tammy, you're in. Bosanka said so."

" 'Bosanka said so,' " she mimicked. "What do I care? I think she's mad. You're all mad."

Something in her tone reminded me of Joel, of all people. Then it dawned on me: the problem was not that Tamsin didn't believe—she was the one with the guru, right? The problem was that she was jealous of me and my "powers." She'd come up with the Comet Committee idea that night, but I was the one who turned out to have been mixed up with wizards and monsters and magic all along. She couldn't stand it.

"Tamsin, listen," I said. "The whole point of Bosanka insisting on help from the Comet Committee instead of just coming to me is that she thinks *all* of us have magic talent. You heard her, Lennie—Mimi? She said that separately we're not much, but together we have the power she needs."

Mimi looked teary-eyed. "I don't want any 'power'! Where does it come from?" She turned pale. "Next time I go to Mass, will my foot sizzle when I step over the threshold of the church?"

"Of course not!" I yelled.

Lennie grabbed Mimi and shook her gently.

"Mimi, come on, calm down," he said. "It's nothing like that." He touched the chain around her neck. "You're wearing a religious medal, right? It hasn't burned you or anything, has it?"

Lennie had spent some time in a Catholic school, so he knew what to say. Mimi began to calm down. Tamsin caught my eye and looked away again, but for one instant we were both on the same wavelength: good for Lennie!

"So where does it come from?" Mimi asked nervously. She clutched her medal-on-a-chain with both hands. "Your power, Val?"

"I don't know," I said. The family talent had come to my attention through my Gran and Paavo Latvela, two people I loved. It just would never occur to me that good people's magic could be evil. "All I can tell you is, I've never seen my family talent used to hurt anybody, except really evil witchy types like Dr. Brightner and his awful wife—and even then, my Gran tried first to get Ushah to come over to our side."

Tamsin inquired coldly, "Tell me something, who decides which people get to use this 'power' and which ones don't?"

"Maybe you have to earn it," Mimi ventured. "Say, like if your great-great-grandfather saved the king's life so all his descendants get to be dukes? It's sort of a reward for brave deeds and things." She smiled timidly.

"Or it could be something like electricity," Lennie said. "If you happen to be born with the right plug designed into your genes, you can learn to tap into this current that's out there."

I said firmly, "I don't know and right now I can't find out, but from what I've seen, if you're a decent person you use your talent for decent things. If you're a creep you do creepy things with it."

"Like Bosanka," Mimi said, with a visible shudder. "She's *horrible*. Even if we can do what she wants, how do we know she'll bring Peter back?"

She was talking to me. I was the expert. Help.

"She has to," I improvised. "She needs us to be the Comet Committee again, and we need Peter in the group. He was here that night. He'll have to be with us on Saturday, if she wants the whole committee's help."

Mimi said, "But I don't want to help her! She's a wicked, awful witch!"

"Wait, think about it a second," Lennie said softly. "She's stuck in a place that's strange to her. She hates it, and she's real scared, I bet. So she makes trouble."

Tamsin said, "Listen, who is this person, anyway? She says she comes from another planet someplace, and she's royalty at home. Really? I mean, what is she? Witchella of Glunkus, or what? How do we know that anything this oddball from nowhere says is true?"

Lennie carefully set his scuffed boots, now shiny with oil, on the floor by his bed. "Tam," he said, "I heard what she said. It sounded right to me. She's for real."

Tamsin said, "What's that supposed to mean?"

"Maybe you don't remember being a foreigner," Lennie said, "but I do."

Tamsin opened her mouth and then shut it and turned to look out the window. And I remembered the first time I'd seen Lennie, with his funny haircut, stumbling through accented English, which he only spoke at all if he absolutely could not avoid talking.

Mimi brightened. "Val, couldn't we bring Peter back ourselves with—with our 'power'?"

I had a strong wrench of longing for Gran, who would know how to do that. But as Mom had said, I wasn't Gran. So I said, "I think we'd better leave that to the person who changed him in the first place."

"Yeah," Tamsin sniped, looking meanly at me, "we don't

want to 'bring him back' halfway, say, because we don't know what we're doing, family gift or no family gift."

"So what's *your* plan, Tam?" Lennie flashed, and she glared and shut up. Lennie turned to me expectantly.

I took a deep breath and laid out my plan, the only plan I could think of. "We *say* we'll help. Bosanka brings Peter back to complete the committee. Then we all grab hands and we use our power against her." I sounded like a comic book supercharacter. If they didn't all laugh me out of the apartment over this, I'd be getting off lightly.

I pushed on. "We make another comet, like we did New Year's Eve, and we wrap it around Bosanka and sling her back into outer space or wherever she came from."

Lennie scratched his neck. "Uh, problem: that girl, Val, the one you didn't recognize? It was Beth Stowers."

"Beth Stowers!" I said. "Beth Stowers from eleven B who got pregnant and had to leave school?"

He nodded. "Her parents sent her to stay with some relatives in Ohio. She left New Year's Day."

Mimi blinked at Lennie. "Wow," she said.

"Hey, it wasn't me!" Lennie blushed.

Tamsin said to him darkly, "You didn't tell me any of this. So what was this Beth doing here on New Year's?"

"She didn't want to see any of her friends," Lennie explained uncomfortably, "but she really didn't want to be all alone with her parents, either. I told her no other kids from her grade would be here. And don't ask me anything more about her because it's none of your business, okay? I had nothing to do with the . . . with the pregnancy part."

Tamsin laughed. "Nobody thinks you're *that* dim."

"You all thought it for a minute there," Lennie mumbled.

I said, "The possibility crossed our minds, Lennie. So what? Relax, will you?"

Suddenly I saw that Lennie cared not only what his

sister thought about him but what *I* thought about him. Just the way I cared what he thought about me. Boy, was I glad he was in this with me!

"Listen," I said, "what we should be worrying about right now is what Bosanka will say when we tell her one of the committee is definitely out."

Lennie said, "Hey, she's not some bug-woman from Betelgeuse, she won't go on a rampage just because of one person."

"Sure, she'll think it's a great story," Tamsin said, eyeing him. "So are *you* going to tell Bosanka about this?"

"I will," I said, with a sinking heart. "I'm her student host."

Tamsin slung her hair again, like a crow shooting out a black wing, and said, "Valentine, if you have these magical connections, 'Sorcery Hall' and everything, why can't you get them to take care of Bosanka?"

"I tried," I said. "No dice. Which isn't so strange, really—I mean, I'm not even a member, and my Gran, who is, can't help. They have their troubles, too, some kind of wizard war they've been fighting for a long time. We have to go on the assumption that we're on our own."

Tamsin said, "Well, why does it have to be such a big deal? Why not just walk away, refuse to cooperate? So this Peter gets to be a deer for the rest of his life. Sounds like he asked for it."

Lennie got up and paced around silently in his socks. "Peter wouldn't have been anywhere near Bosanka if he wasn't with me in the first place. I let him hang around because he's, you know, such a loner, such a—"

"A dork," I said.

Everybody giggled.

I said, "He's a dork, Lennie, we all know that. It doesn't make what's happened to him any better, but it's been true since he started at Jefferson and it's still true. If he hadn't blasted off with his moron mouth, this never would have happened to him."

Tamsin interrupted impatiently. "He's not even the real problem. Nobody's using their heads here. What if we do find Bosanka's people for her? I mean, what's to stop them from taking over everything, if they've all got magic powers? Maybe they've just been waiting for her to come and lead their conquest of Earth, unless we stop her."

"We?" Tamsin was in, and I was beginning to wish she'd stayed out after all. She sounded like paranoid Peter, but worse—witch-invaders instead of Red Hordes.

"Well, what if?" she demanded, striking what they call in ballet an "attitude." She didn't believe this theory of hers at all, she was just stirring up trouble.

Mimi the suggestible picked up on it right away. "Oh, God! Bosanka said her own world was ruined, didn't she? They don't have a home anymore. And they're here already, just waiting to move in on us!"

"Wait a minute, wait," I said, waving my hands. "Nobody said we were going to do what she wants in the first place, remember? We *pretend* we're going to signal her people for her, but what we're really going to do is get rid of her—return to sender."

"How? You couldn't stop her from turning Peter into a deer," Mimi accused me. "You didn't even try."

"Not just me," I said. "All of us. The Comet Committee."

Mimi said, "You mean take on a whole race of secret aliens? Just us?"

"Not if we can help it," I said.

Tamsin said, "And what if we can't help it? What if she's just too much for us, with her people or without them, and we have to do what she wants?"

"Then we are all in big fat trouble," I said, "but since

93

we're already all in big fat trouble, what difference does it make?"

I was running out of patience. My own share of the big, fat trouble was weighing heavily on my mind, starting with the fact that somehow I had to get hold of Joel and convince him that he was in, too.

10

Leather Walls

Instead of going to school the next day I took the air shuttle to Boston. Mom paid for my ticket with a credit card at a machine downtown, and promised to call in an excuse for me at school.

"Do you want me to go to the plane with you?" she said.

"No, Mom," I said. Good grief, did she think I was still twelve?

"I don't know why you can't do all the research you need for your paper here in New York," she said.

But she didn't push it. I hated the way my silver wish made Mom go softheaded whenever she got close to what I was doing. But it was better than having her keep me from doing it.

She told me to have a good trip and not to talk to strangers, and she left me at the stop for the airport bus. I haven't flown much, but I was too tired to be scared. In fact, I fell asleep. When we landed, a guy a few seats ahead of me took from the overhead bin what I recognized as some kind of an instrument case. I worked up my nerve and asked him about it.

Not only was he a musician (a flute player, it turned out), he was a faculty member at Joel's school. He commuted to Boston three times a week from New York where he lived and played with a wind ensemble. He showed me how to get into town from the airport on a special subway.

Downtown Boston struck me as a version of lower Manhattan, but with more red brick. Cleaner, too. Boston Common, which the flute teacher pointed out to me as we passed it, looked small inside its iron fence. I wondered if it had park magic, like Central Park.

We shared a cab to the school, a huge old building like a castle that leaked music at every seam. The flute teacher dropped me at the main office. I asked where I could wait to catch Joel between classes. The guy behind the desk said Joel wasn't around.

In fact Joel hadn't been in school today, or yesterday, either. If I wanted to see him I would have to get in touch with his uncle, Abraham Wechsler. The man at the desk, Mr. Rush, asked me if I had the address.

I said I did, wondering out loud how much longer it would take to locate Joel, because it was important.

"He isn't at his uncle's," Mr. Rush said. "I guess you don't know, is that right? About Joel?"

"*What* about Joel?" I said, utterly clutched.

Mr. Rush ran his palm over the bald top of his head and sighed. "He's more or less withdrawn himself from student life here," he began, and then I guess my stunned look got through. He added hastily, "I probably shouldn't tell you this, but everybody in school knows anyway. Joel has signed himself into a mental hospital. He's been sending away anybody who tries to visit him, but maybe a talk with a friend from home is just what he needs."

So that's how I came to visit the Minuteman Psychiatric Center. The place was on the outskirts of the city, which I reached via the Boston subway and by talking to a lot of strangers (sorry, Mom) to get directions.

The grounds were enclosed in a wall made of designer cinderblock in pale green. At the tall front gates a uniformed man in a little kiosk stopped me. He took down my name and passed me through with a visitor's badge pinned to my coat collar.

The inside was not what I expected. No iron bars, no straightjacketed inmates parked on benches to take the sun, only a gardener clipping a hedge and a couple of women in ugly white nurse shoes walking together and consulting over a clipboard in front of a long, two-story brick building.

By now it was lunchtime. The receptionist in the front office suggested that I go look for Joel in the cafeteria, where I found a scattering of ordinary-looking types eating at plastic tables.

Looking more closely I noticed how one guy sat moving his plate and his plastic fork and his cup around (trying to get them into some sort of crucial alignment, I guess) while his spaghetti cooled. And there was a girl about my age who sucked her thumb instead of eating. Otherwise, it was nothing special. Usual cafeteria smell: awful.

I consulted the nearest person with a name badge on. She said Joel would be in the West Lounge watching television.

Daytime television? Joel? Joel the snob, the compulsive practicer? What had they done, lobotomized him? I hurried down the corridor. Through open doorways I caught glimpses of beds and chairs and people sitting in little rooms. Clashing waves of radio music wafted into the hallway.

I found Joel, in pajama pants and a sweatshirt, in front

of the TV as promised. He sat in a plastic chair, hunched over with his chin on his fists, apparently watching cartoons. A girl with frizzy hair was also watching, sitting on the floor. She looked at me out of the corners of her eyes.

"Joel," I said.

"What?" He swung around to face me, banging his hands down on his knees. "I said I didn't want—"

He looked absolutely awful, like an actor playing a bum, with stubbly cheeks and circles under his eyes.

"*Shit!*" he said, and he jumped up and grabbed my wrist.

"Hey, hold it, what—"

"Shush, the place is full of nuts and their keepers," he said. "Come on, we'll try the pit."

"What pit?" I said, yanking my hand free.

He said, "Relax. If you turn purple they start paying attention to you."

So we walked, in tense silence, to what turned out to be the Minuteman Center's padded cell. It was a small, empty room with thick brown leather mats all over the walls, floor, and ceiling. One window had steel mesh over the inside.

"So you can't get to the glass," Joel said. "Glass cuts. They worry a lot about suicide in here."

I stood in the middle of the room, not wanting to touch any part of it. Now that I was there, I couldn't think of anything to say.

Joel shut the padded door behind us. "Who told you where to find me?" he said.

"A guy at your school. In the administration office."

"Mostly bald, kind of sweet?"

"Uh, yeah—"

"Ted Rush," he said.

" 'Kind of sweet'?" I said.

He gave me this sardonic look. I could tell he was

reading my thoughts and finding them, to say the least, wanting.

He said, "Ted's a nice guy. I like him, period. Look, in the music world, which is full of family men and women by the way, you get used to gay people. I've had to make my position clear since I was pretty young, and my position is that I'm just not inclined that way. So Ted Rush is nothing special, okay? What did he say, anyway?"

"He said I could find you here," I mumbled, feeling unfairly chastened. Embarrassment made me irritable. "Joel, what are you doing in this place? I thought you said you'd rather die than get stuck in some hospital!"

"I'm not stuck," he said. "I signed myself in here and I can sign myself out."

"But why did you sign yourself in?"

"I failed my auditions." He pushed away from the door and began to pace.

"What auditions?" I asked. "You're still in music school, how can you have auditions?"

"Auditions for the school orchestra," he said.

"I thought you wanted to be a soloist."

"I do," he said impatiently, "but being in the student orchestra is important. Real conductors come and work with you. You learn a whole lot."

"And they didn't let you in?"

He sniffed and said with wounded dignity, "Into the B orchestra, yes. Not the A orchestra."

"There are two of them?"

"Of course there are; the school has too many students for just one orchestra."

"Well, what's so terrible about the B orchestra?"

"B orchestra," he snarled. "Second twelve. Not even in the first twelve chairs. *Second twelve.*"

"Okay," I said, giving up, "so this terrible thing hap-

99

pened. How does signing yourself into a nuthouse get you into the A orchestra instead?"

He scowled. "I wanted some time alone, quiet, away from everybody. Huh. Little did I know. You'd be amazed how much the crazy people get on your nerves."

"I can imagine," I said, thinking of the girl sucking her thumb and the guy making a maze out of his lunch.

Somebody bumped the door from outside. Joel sat down with his back against it. "No lock," he explained. "Not on this side, anyway. They leave it open. That way, if you're suddenly taken with a violent need to be violent, you come in here and put some dents in the padding instead of in your roommate."

"You have a roommate in here?" I said.

Joel nodded. "Do I ever. He hasn't said a single word to anybody in seven months. He hums, though. I have explained to the kind and helpful staff that I am *trying* to become a musician, and that either he stops humming or they get me another roommate or I kill him, one of the above, take your pick. They're working on it. While they work on it, I hang out at the TV. The soaps are brain dead, but some of the cartoons aren't bad."

"Glad to hear it," I said. "Joel, what are you really doing here?"

He grinned. "Well, I'm crazy or I wouldn't be locked up, right? I told you all about it, before New Year's."

There was something funny about the way he looked at me: straight, open, honest, and totally false. Like at the coffee shop on Columbus, where I'd sensed from the beginning that he was keeping something crucial about all this to himself.

I said, "You told me you were having trouble playing the violin because of your hands, but you didn't sound particularly crazy."

100

"You remember," he said. "It's nice to know that even as a crazy person one can make a mark on the world."

"Are you still having the same problems?" I said.

"Fits," he said, looking away from me again. Evasive, that was the word. And scared. Scared to tell me—what? What could it be? "Sometimes," he said.

"What do they say about your hands here?"

He shrugged. "I haven't told them anything about that. It's my problem, not theirs. All they know is that I can't concentrate on my studies, as my audition failure shows, and that I've been driving my aunt and uncle crazy. Big deal. Breakdowns are common up here."

I chewed that over without comment. It certainly was very silent in the padded room.

"Well?" he said. "Aren't you going to ask me how they can cure me if I don't tell them what's really wrong? The answer is that if they knew what's really bothering me they'd decide I wasn't just a 'high-strung adolescent' but an honest-to-goodness loon, and they'd get to work trying to cure me, which they can't do. I would never get out of here, and that isn't the point at all."

I made myself stay patient. "So what is the point?"

"I told you: peace and quiet, a kind of retreat."

"Why didn't you just hole up at your uncle's place for a while?"

"Guilt," he said. "Everybody wants to help. Aunt Matty keeps trying to fix me up with daughters of friends of hers. She thinks I'm having trouble making a 'social adjustment' and I need more friends. My uncle knows that's not a problem, but then what is? So he's also worried. The two of them get on my nerves, so I'm always snapping their heads off. That's not peace and quiet for anybody."

"Who's paying for this?" I said, giving the leather padding a thump. "It must be costing somebody a whole bunch of money to keep you here."

"More guilt," he said stonily. "Thanks. My family is paying. I intend to make it up to them as soon as I start earning a living."

"How long are you planning to stay?"

"As long as I have to." I thought I saw a flash of panic, but he got up and turned restlessly away from me. "You're supposed to be at school."

"I didn't come up just to visit," I began, but he interrupted me, his voice rising.

"Well, I don't give a damn why you did come because I sure did not ask you to. I am not asking you to leave, either; I'm telling you. I don't particularly enjoy you sitting there in your cute jeans and sweater and quilted coat staring at me in my goddamn jammies and a stinking sweatshirt with food stains on it. So beat it, Val. I'm not in the mood to entertain guests."

"No, you're in the mood to be miserable and indulge your lousy 'temperament,'" I said. "You get a lot of mileage out of being 'high-strung,' Joel. I've let you tell me your sad story. Now it's my turn, okay?"

"What are you yelling about?" he said in an injured tone.

"I am really fed up with everybody going off in emotional flares around me all the time." Like him and Mimi and Tamsin, and for that matter Bosanka herself. I was beginning to long for a straightforward slimy monster or rogue wizard. "Everybody else gets to be temperamental and I get to be good old solid Val who holds it all together. Well, forget it. You can save your suffering for the staff here, that's their job. With me, you can please just shut up and listen for a minute."

He leaned back on the padded door again, trying to look cool and bored.

I crossed my arms, steadying myself. "I told you part of it already. Then you hung up on me, remember? Bosanka Lonat says the Comet Committee has some kind of psychic power which she wants to commandeer to contact her own people, who are here someplace but she can't find them, not without our help. So she needs the Comet Committee. And Bosanka says the Comet Committee includes you."

Silence. Joel waited, looking down at his dirty sneakers.

I said, "I know you think the Comet Committee is a lot of bull, but you'd better start taking it seriously. Bosanka does. She's already turned one guy on the committee into a deer because we weren't all together yesterday after school. Now we've got till Saturday. I don't know what will happen if we don't all show up, but it won't be fun. We need you."

Joel said, "If they have this place bugged, you're in deep, deep trouble."

I said, "You were with me when this all started, Joel. We did magic together, you and me and Paavo. But this time there's no Paavo and Gran's maybe dying. This is too much for me, okay? I need you."

"No, you don't," he said firmly. "You've done fine without me all along."

I looked as hard as I could right into his eyes and I said, "Okay, forget it. I'm sorry I asked. You fooled me, that time you took on the kraken's punks in the park. I thought you had guts."

He had started pacing again. I followed him around the little room, talking. I was mad.

"But you hung up on me when I told you a little bit about Bosanka, and now you're hiding here. This isn't because of any B orchestra. It's because of the Comet Committee. You were dying for Paavo to teach you, you moan and groan about not having any magic of your own, but you're hiding out from magic. You're a coward, and Paavo would be ashamed of you. *I* sure am."

Joel whirled around and punched the leather-padded wall with both fists.

"*Okay,*" he said.

It's embarrassing when a smart person's buttons are so easy to push.

11

Committed

They told Joel to request his release in writing. He scribbled on a paper napkin, "Let me out of here. Joel Wechsler."

We waited an hour, which I used to fill Joel in on the details. He listened without saying much of anything, avoiding my eyes. I still didn't know *why*.

Finally a doctor sat down with us and asked who I was, and who I was did not cut it. He said he would have to talk to some other people before letting Joel out.

I said, "I thought you had to let him leave if he asked to go."

The doctor, who had a stringy red beard and looked as if he needed somebody to fatten him up a little, said, "There are complicating factors which I think I should only discuss with the immediate family, Miss Marsh."

Joel, keeping his cool with superhuman effort, said, "Val, don't waste your time, go home. I'll get this straightened out and come to New York as fast as I can."

So I went back home and fell on my bed, exhausted. To keep from going crazy, I worked on an old story I'd done in last year's creative writing class about waking up to find yourself in a loony bin. I ended up throwing the whole story out, it was so hopeless.

Joel called after dinner. "You're not going to believe this," he said in a strained voice. "When you commit yourself around here, you are really *committed*."

Doom, doom, doom, my heart drummed. "What?" I said.

"It turns out that if they have reason to believe that you might be dangerous to yourself or anybody else, they can hold you here while they set up a sanity hearing before a couple of doctors who get to decide whether it's safe to let you out or not."

"That's nuts!" I yelled into the phone.

"Very funny, Val," Joel said sarcastically.

"When is this hearing?" I said.

"Not till next week at least," he answered. "Judges and doctors don't like to give up their weekend golf."

"Oh, no," I said.

"I'm sorry." He sounded miserable. "It's my own fault. Remember when I called you up and blew off about the state of the world? I talked pretty much the same way here the other night, trying to get through to that jerk, my roommate. I got through, all right. He passed on my remarks to somebody on the staff here, thus thrilling them all with *their* success in breaking his silence. Meantime, the shrinks are afraid that I'm so depressed if they let me out I'll lie down in front of a train, and then my parents will sue them."

"God, Joel!"

"I probably should go lie down in front of a train," he

added gloomily. "When my parents hear that I've got to have a sanity hearing to get out of here, they *are* going to kill me."

"Don't talk like that," I said. "If someone overhears you, it'll make things worse!"

He chortled without humor. "If? I'm calling from the patients' pay phone, and there's actually a member of the staff keeping an eye on me in case I try to strangle myself with the phone wire. *Gak, gak.*"

"Listen, Joel. If you're stuck, you're stuck. I'll explain to —everybody. Don't do anything to get yourself locked up there forever, all right? We'll just have to manage without you."

"Not this time!" he said harshly and hung up.

So Joel still hadn't gotten over missing the climax of the kraken affair. Now he would probably try something desperate and get himself locked away for years, and there was no way I could stop him.

There was no way I could produce him at Bosanka's Comet Committee meeting on Saturday, either.

I didn't call Lennie or anybody about my failure to get Joel out. I punished myself instead by doing a load of assigned reading about the Civil War, which seemed about as connected to my life as the canals on Mars and took enough light-years to plow through that I felt like I'd traveled to Mars and back by the time I finished.

The next morning, Friday, Bosanka sat on the other side of our homeroom, ignoring me. It did not seem like a good time to insist on conversation, not with what I had to tell her. So I waited.

We spent the day avoiding each other, but sooner or later I was going to have to face her with the bad news. Sooner or later might be my last moments at the Thomas Jefferson School, or anywhere.

Lennie was in the language lab at lunchtime, listening to tapes of whales and dolphins for his "Spaceship Earth" project. "Hey, Val," he said excitedly, "did I tell you my dad is trying to fix up a place for me in a research lab in Hawaii in the spring? Working with dolphins!"

"Terrific," I said with attempted enthusiasm. I hated to bring him down, but if I didn't get somebody else down there with me, I was going to go crazy. I squeezed into the little lab cubby with him. "Bad news," I said. "Joel put himself into a nut-hatch in Boston and they won't let him out."

Lennie closed his eyes. "Oh boy," he said. "Well, here's *my* bad news: Mimi's gone."

"Gone!" I said. "Gone where?"

"I don't know." He fiddled anxiously with the head-set, which was making faint booms, squeaks, and whis-tling noises. "Her sister says she's run away."

I groaned. "How can we fight Bosanka if we can't even hold the stupid committee together? What about this 'team' you said we had here?"

He hung his head. "Hey, calm down, Val. I thought we were okay, honest. I guess I was wrong. Look, Bosanka's going to be at the drama club rehearsal today, a kid in the club told me. I'll meet you there. We'll tell her together."

"Hey, Lennie," I said. "Thanks. Really."

He blushed and put his headset back on.

I had one free period to kill until drama club so I wandered the halls, noting the little details as if it were my last day on earth (which it might well be): one long blue sock lying outside 10B's homeroom; some seniors having a raisin fight in the east side stairwell. Funny to think that after so many years of school and all my hard work, there was a chance I might not survive to graduate.

The place erupted, as usual, at the period break. A tall kid with earphones on (strictly against school rules) bopped backward down the hall. People greeted each other with shouts and whoops: "Dominic! Wait up!" "Julie!" "Hi, *dude*!" "What's Wayne doing over *there*?"

Two girls pushed past, heads close together. "Come on, tell me who it was," one of them said, elbowing the other one in the ribs.

"No, I can't."

"Well, don't tell me her name, then, just give me a hint."

In the girls' room, some sophomores were at the mirrors over the sinks. I hid in one of the booths, the Phantom of the High School.

"I *hate* my nose."

"I hate *my* nose."

"Your nose is okay, it's cute."

"What kind of eyeliner is that? Let me try it?"

I could hear them jostling and giggling.

"My sister hates *her* nose."

"Why? It's not so bad."

"Shhh. You're not supposed to say anything about it or she gets real upset."

How come they get to compare noses and I get to tackle an ice princess from another planet?

The bell rang and the halls emptied out. Wandering around, I found Barb on the third floor putting up her photographs. She was going great guns in the school photography club this term, using the ancient Leica she'd been given for Christmas. She'd been asked to put up the best prints from her stay in Barbados with her aunt, who was a doctor down there.

"Nice pictures," I said, admiring shots of a muscular kid clowning on a beat-up-looking boat. "Who's he?"

"Cousin," she said through a mouthful of pushpins.

"You know what?" I said. "You were right. My foreign guest is bad, bad news."

Barb considered this while she went on placing pictures. When I tried to help she snapped at me, insisting that I only touch the white edges so I wouldn't get any fingerprints on the photographic prints. Some of these pictures did not even have white edges.

"Bad, bad news, huh? Like what?" she said finally.

My best friend should at least have some idea of why I didn't make it to graduation. I told her all while she finished arranging her pictures.

"Peter *Weiss*?" she crowed. "Into a deer? I've got some people this girl has just got to meet!"

"Seriously," I said, "that dork Peter is running around on all fours in Central Park with hooves, horns, and a flippy little tail."

Barb said, "How come she didn't turn him into one of these leaf-taker things, like the store clerk?"

"I have a theory about that," I said. "I think the longer she's away from her own home the shakier her memory gets. That thing isn't a 'leaf-taker.' It has a name in Bosanka's own language, but she couldn't remember it. Everything's fading, which is why she's so frantic to get to her people before it all goes."

Barb studied the arrangement of her photos. "Maybe that's why she's making pictures of her native animals in Central Park, trying to keep it all alive for herself as long as she can. And I've noticed some other funny things in the park lately— lines of little stones, twigs stuck in the ground to make patterns. I know people who would take one look and say it was juju."

"Juju?" I said, stunned. "Barb, are you saying you *believe* me?"

"Valentine, you may be a stuck-up fool sometimes, but you've never been a liar—not to me, anyway." Barb looked up and down the corridor; we were alone. "That time you came bombing into my mom's shop with Ushah the Awful after you?"

"I remember," I said. "If you hadn't helped me, I never would have escaped in one piece."

"My hand-mirror that I gave you that afternoon?" she said. "The one that helped you rescue your mom? I kept the little piece you gave me back afterward. I thought I could see special things in there. Wishful thinking, I told myself. But I kept that piece of glass with me.

"Well, I showed it to somebody in Barbados, a juju man Aunt Ruth knows. He said he could see traces of strong magic inside the glass, so something big had happened around my mirror, just like you told me yourself.

"Now I saw this man do things you wouldn't believe— well, maybe you would, with your magic Gran and all. So yeah, I believe that my mirror helped you beat an evil wizard. And if you tell me now that Bosanka is harassing this committee of yours, I believe that too."

I felt my heart thump and my eyes get big. "You mean you've seen some magic yourself, in Barbados?"

"Oh, a couple of things," she said nonchalantly. "Tell you all about it sometime, when you got a minute. But first, what are you going to do about Bosanka?"

Back to the horrible here and now. I sighed. "Lennie and I are going to ask her for more time, today, at drama club. I don't know what will happen. She's so crazy and arrogant—!"

"Indeed," Barb said dryly. She shut her photo portfolio and fished her camera out of her backpack. "Good thing I've got this with me today."

"Why?" I said.

"To take to the auditorium, of course," she said. "I want to get some shots of this royal witch of yours."

I had heavy, scary, second thoughts. "Listen, Bosanka

may be hazy about the details of her home magic but she's still dynamite. I mean, she's dangerous, Barb!"

"Valentine, I understand that," she said sweetly. "I'm the one who gets the A's, remember?"

"Okay," I said, in a burst of creative annoyance, "so how about standing in for Beth Stowers in the Comet Committee? Then I can tell Bosanka that I've got a replacement, and maybe we won't get killed on the spot."

Barb hooked her arm through mine and we headed for the auditorium together. "I thought you'd never ask."

Lennie met us outside the big double doors.

"Barb is joining the Comet Committee in Beth's place," I said. "That's one down!"

Lennie solemnly shook Barb's hand.

We slipped inside and sat down in back. The drama club was rehearsing a modernized *Hamlet*. Kim Larkin, the school clique queen, was Ophelia, and gorgeous Michael Scott (the senior heartthrob who had completely slipped my mind lately for obvious reasons) was Hamlet.

To my utter amazement, Bosanka was reading the part of Queen Gertrude, Hamlet's mother. I could not believe it! Lennie quickly got the story from his friend and passed the word on to Barb, who passed it to me. The girl playing Gertrude had failed a crucial chem test, so she was busy being tutored for a makeup. Mr. Fischer, the drama club's faculty advisor, had somehow or other ended up letting Bosanka pinch-hit as the queen.

I bet he had no idea why he did that.

Barb slipped off down the side aisle with her camera in her hand. I stayed put in the back row, feeling ravenous with tension.

Michael declaimed, "Now, mother, what's the matter?"

Bosanka read from some mimeographed sheets in her hand. "Hamlet, thou hast thy father much offended." The

112

effect was amazing. It didn't matter how square and plain she was. She was the Snow Queen, lofty and cool, with Hamlet dithering around somewhere about knee level.

My friend Megan sat down next to me. "Wow," she whispered, "what an actress! I should have signed up for a foreign guest, too, though with my luck, I'd get some nerd. What's she like, really?"

"What wilt thou do?" said Bosanka with cool disdain. "Thou wilt not murder me?"

"What you see," I said, "is what you get."

"My mom is always yakking about 'really strong women,' you know?" Megan said. "She should meet Bosanka."

Was this Megan talking? Megan who had been madly in love for years with a boy who treated her like a wad of gum stuck to his shoe?

But she was right, Bosanka was impressive as the completely unruffled monarch of all she surveyed. Poor Michael was just part of the survey. On the stage with Bosanka, he was a mere cute boy saying words he didn't really understand very well.

"O, speak to me no more," Bosanka said, "spurning" him, that was the only term for it. She sat down in the lone wooden chair on the stage and gazed coldly up at him. "These words like daggers enter in mine ears. No more, sweet Hamlet."

Even Mr. Fischer was impressed. I could tell by the polite way he talked to her. Fischer, who usually prowled the balcony roaring, "I'm not convinced! *Convince* me!"

He said, "Gertrude, I think you could be more *upset* when you do this scene. The queen as a proud, powerful woman who follows her own will and isn't used to being criticized is very effective. It will work even better if she falters here and lets what Hamlet says really get to her. Would you try that approach, please?"

He was treating her the way a real director treats a real actress—a star.

Every single person in that auditorium was watching her while Michael, bemused, fished out his line and delivered it. It wasn't his fault that he barely existed up there. He was on stage pretending to be a prince with a person who was royal without having to pretend.

"Alas, he's mad," said Bosanka contemptuously.

Royal and threatening. She had a ruthless streak a mile wide, something to do with being "highborn" in a place that I was beginning to suspect had been pretty rough, tough, and basic, no matter how magical. Her brutal simplicity came through, making her Queen Gertrude absolutely convincing.

She was removed from everybody else. You could see it in the way the other kids treated her. They deferred to her, but nobody kidded around with her the way friends do. They wouldn't shout her name in the hall or ask her how she liked or didn't like her nose. She was only playing at being one of them, and they sensed it.

No wonder she was so desperate to get back to "her people." We were not them.

Megan said in an awed whisper, "You know what she's got? She's got *presence*."

"Why, look you there!" Michael yelped. "Look how it steals away! My father, in his habit as he lived! Look where he goes even now out at the portal!"

Mr. Fischer, standing in for the ghost, tiptoed away.

Bosanka said icily to Michael, "This is the very coinage of your brain. This bodiless creation ecstasy is very cunning in." I don't think any of us knew what the heck "ecstasy" meant in that sentence, including Bosanka. It didn't matter a bit. Michael cringed.

"Excellent!" shouted Fischer. "Let's stop there, everybody, for today." He talked briefly with Bosanka and then walked out with Michael, the two of them intent on some line-reading or other. Not that advice from Fischer or anybody else would make much difference.

Bosanka stood on the stage holding a long wooden dowel used as a sword in the duel scenes. She gave the side curtain a quick, vicious, capable-looking jab with it.

When we were alone with her, I went down front with Lennie. Close by I could hear Barb's camera snick.

First the good news. "Bosanka," I quavered, "we need to talk with you. We've been working on getting the whole committee together for you tomorrow. Beth Stowers just is not available, but we have a replacement, somebody who really belongs in the Comet Committee."

Her pale eyes narrowed with suspicion. "Who?"

"My friend Barbara Wilson," I said.

Bosanka pointed the dowel at Barb. "That one?"

"Yes, that's Barbara—"

The dowel whistled down and cracked against the back of the chair they had been using in the scene. The chair screamed. I mean *screamed*, a high-pitched shriek that left my ears ringing and my heart paralyzed.

Bosanka roared, "Should be you I hit! Or this walking darkness, witch of the left hand, night demon!"

"What, what?" I stammered. I squinted at the chair. Had it really moved in a creaking flinch under the whiplash blow of the stick? "Demon? Who?"

"Me," Barb said loudly. "She means 'black.' "

"Black, black, black!" Bosanka yelled. She stamped on the stage, which boomed like a drum. "Even here you say it—black magic!"

Which goes to show that I had just not taken Barb's objections seriously enough. After all, how did racial prejudice fit in with royalty from another world? The plain fact is,

I forgot there might be a problem, and Barb had not reminded me. Maybe she'd hoped, deep down, that she was wrong.

There was no more room for doubt.

"The girl is crazy," Barb announced in trembling fury. "You-all will excuse me if I take my wicked black self out of here so as not to lose my terrible left-hand temper and tear off somebody's head."

I ran after her. Behind me I heard Lennie talking soothingly to Bosanka. Was he crazy? What do you say to a magical savage who is also a raving bigot?

Barb and I burst out of the auditorium together.

"What's going on?" said Mrs. Denby, nimbly skipping out of our way. "Who's in the auditorium, girls?"

"Imperial Wizard of the Ku Klux Klan," Barb snapped, and stalked off.

I panted, "Um, just rehearsing, Mrs. Denby. We'll be through soon."

"Valentine," she said, "you know students aren't supposed to be in the building after classes without a faculty advisor. Didn't Mr. Fischer just leave?"

"Uh, yes." How could I stop Mrs. Denby from going into the auditorium? A student turned into a deer was one thing, but the assistant principal?

Mrs. Denby studied me with her well-known X-ray eyes. "What's going on here?"

"Just a rehearsal," I said. Paavo Latvela had once commented, ambiguously, on my talent for lying. He would have been proud of me now. "We're doing a skit demonstrating the meaning of the First Amendment. Barb came to take some publicity stills."

Mrs. Denby said, "Really," and walked past me into the auditorium. I plunged in after her.

The place was empty—nothing, nobody, just the chair up on the stage.

"What's all the mystery about?" Mrs. Denby asked.

"Uh, what mystery? There's no mystery, Mrs. D."

"You kids," she said, and she marched out.

I jumped onto the stage. The chair, made of ancient, bescribbled school oak, had a jagged crack down the center of its upper back-support. Rough little beads of pale, sticky stuff oozed down into a small puddle of what looked like varnish on the hardwood stage below.

That old oak chair, after years of drying out in classrooms and storerooms, was bleeding fresh sap from where Bosanka had whipped it.

12

Vandals and Huns

I found Lennie outside on the school steps. "Where'd you go?" I said. "You scared me to death!"

"Out the side door to the other corridor," he said. "Ssshh, look."

Bosanka stood with Michael Scott at the school's front steps: trucklike, booted Bosanka and the beautiful Michael in stone-washed jeans, golden curls, and mountaineer parka. A distressing sight.

I turned back to Lennie. "Are you okay?" I said. "After what she did to that chair—"

"Don't remind me," he said painfully. "She opened up whole new possibilities that I don't want to think about. Like, what life was like in her world for the people who weren't 'highborn,' or who weren't even people, to her."

"Let alone the animal life," I said.

"I know," Lennie said, wincing. He had always been sensitive about the sufferings of other creatures.

But I was wound up, I just couldn't stop. "All that stuff about hunting—in the sea and the air—maybe they tore their forests apart, too. Maybe all their plants had consciousness that a 'highborn' like Bosanka could wake with her magic and abuse whenever she felt like it! The girl is a total *barbarian*, the Huns and the Vandals all wrapped up in one big package."

He started to say something—maybe a defense of Bosanka, as he'd defended her before—but just then Michael and Bosanka started walking away.

"Come on," I said. "We still have to talk to her."

"Right now?" Lennie said, hanging back. "I don't know, Val. She's pretty upset."

"Listen, Lennie," I said, "even Bosanka might soften up after spending time with Michael Scott. I mean, she is a girl, right? And you have to admit, Michael is gorgeous."

"And he's walking around with a lethal person," Lennie said with a sideways look at me. "You think us being around will protect him from her bad temper?"

"Who knows," I muttered. "Come on." The thing about your good friends is that they know you so well—even the parts you don't particularly want them to know.

We followed Bosanka and Michael to the park through the chilly afternoon. Bosanka didn't have any books for him to carry for her. She didn't need props.

"How come she didn't turn you into a deer or something?" I asked Lennie.

He zipped his parka shut. The afternoon sunshine didn't have much warmth in it. "I don't know," he said finally. "I said to her, 'Look, we have to talk about this, and I can't talk if you turn me into a dumb animal.' She said, 'You are already dumb animal,' and stomped out."

Lennie had a lot of guts, but if I said so I knew he'd get all embarrassed, so I didn't. Privately I thought he was amazing.

"Not that there aren't animals that could talk to you, if you could just crack their code," he went on. "My dolphin project is about some scientists who are teaching dolphins to talk. Well, communicate, anyway."

I said, "Sounds great."

"They let you swim with them in the tank," Lennie said, warming to his theme. "On Saturday afternoons, when the training sessions are over for the week."

Up ahead of us, Michael and Bosanka walked the length of Rumsey Playground. No point trying to talk to her with Michael around, and she was obviously in no hurry to get rid of him. We were going to have to be patient. This is not my strong point. Lennie is one of the most patient people I know. We have had our differences about this.

"I hope they'll let me into this project," he said worriedly, "even though I'm only in high school. At least my ear infection is clearing up, but what if they don't want to take any chances with it?"

"They'll let you in," I said automatically.

Behind the arbor at the end of the playground, we found Michael and Bosanka rehearsing *Hamlet* together on the little stage of the concrete band shell. They paid no attention to us or to the guy with a push broom who was sweeping up trash in the seating area. Lennie and I wandered around, keeping an eye on the band shell.

I noticed some pebbles lined up in long wavelike lines across the pavement—just before the push broom wiped out the pattern. Barb had said something about peculiar designs turning up in the park—juju. Could this have something to do with Bosanka?

If it did, the clean-up guy had just swept up a mess of magic without even knowing it.

If only we could deal with Bosanka herself as easily as that!

We walked over toward the statue on the southwest side, two eagles with flapping wings fighting over a small, droopy, obviously dead sheep. There are a lot of statues on predatory themes in Central Park—the stalking puma crouched above the East Drive, the falconer over by Strawberry Fields, the Indian and his dog hunting at the foot of the Mall. No wonder the First Hunter felt at home here.

"Lennie," I said, "I'm really sorry about all this."

He said, "Hey, it's okay. Gives me something to think about now that I've started swimming laps again."

"I'm serious," I said.

Lennie looked surprised. "Me, too," he said. "Swimming laps is boring."

"You don't understand," I insisted. "What if this is all happening to teach me a lesson for thinking I was special, having the family talent and everything?"

"To teach you a lesson?" he said thoughtfully. "What about the rest of us, and whatever talent we've each got?" He hesitantly put his arm around my shoulders and gave me his best werewolf grin. "Don't be so nervous, okay? You're scaring me. Let's figure out what we can say to Bosanka."

Up on the band-shell stage, Michael waved his arms and declaimed while Bosanka prowled around with her mimeographed pages flapping in her hand: the fake prince and the real "highborn," who was impulsive, violent, implacable— like a true aristocrat of olden times, I guess. The real thing without the romance people added later, and the real thing was powerful and ruthless.

I looked at the fighting eagles. That was how we would

have to be—red in tooth and claw—if we were going to be able to stand up to her.

I said, "Lennie, we're changing the plan. We've got to get Bosanka cooled out about the missing people from the committee, and persuade her to let Barb in and to give us more time to wait for Joel and locate Mimi. Then, when Bosanka does call the committee together, we all concentrate on making a sort of laser out of our power and—and use it on her."

Lennie's eyes widened. "You mean—incinerate her?"

"Well, I wouldn't say that, exactly," I backtracked. "But—well—yeah, something like that. We've got to stop her, Lennie. I don't know how else to do it."

He moved away from me, frowning. "I thought we were going to try to send her back where she came from."

My mouth was suddenly dry. I was as scared of what I was saying as I was of Bosanka, because I had an awful feeling that what I was proposing we could actually do, if we put our minds and wills to it. And it was horrible.

I said, "We've got to be hard-nosed about this. She's as wild as these eagles in the statue, Lennie. If we can't stop her or hold out against her and she hooks up with her people, wherever they are, they really could take over, just like Mimi said."

"Everybody knows Mimi's a ditz," Lennie pointed out.

"Sure," I said, "but even a ditz can be right. Look at Bosanka up there! Would she settle for being just a regular person? Did you hear her say those lines? Did you hear that—that chair screech? She's worse than the Huns and the Vandals! She's a natural bully, a tyrant—she'll want to be queen of the world!"

"Well, then," Lennie said patiently, "why doesn't she just do it, if she has that kind of power?"

"Because she doesn't," I said, "not on her own, or she

wouldn't need us. But what about these 'people' of hers? What if they're all like her? And how long have they been here? How much do they know, and who knows anything about them? Everybody worries about nuclear war, but who's seriously on the lookout for a bunch of aliens smart enough to fit right in? Even Bosanka hasn't been able to find them! We have no choice. We've got to take her by surprise and hit as hard as we can—make a, what do they call it? A preemptive strike."

"You sound like Peter," he said.

"So maybe Peter's not completely crazy," I growled. I'd come up with this plan and I hated it. It didn't help a bit that Lennie obviously hated it, too.

He quoted, his pained-looking eyes on Bosanka and Michael up on the stage, " 'What wilt thou do? Thou wilt not murder me?' "

"Self-defense isn't murder!" I said. "Lennie, if she didn't need us, she'd wipe us out without a thought."

"There's got to be something else we can do," he said stubbornly. Lennie is competitive in sports, but in every other way he is one of the gentlest, least aggressive people I know. Maybe because he's really strong, he doesn't have to be all macho.

Normally I really appreciated this quality in him. Now it made me feel like a monster by contrast—but a monster who was *right*. However awful I was, Bosanka was a lot worse. This was not the time to get all squeamish about her.

Lennie walked back to the band shell, head down, shoulders slumped, and I followed.

Some team, I thought bitterly. There's me, and there's the rest of them. Nobody in the committee had had any experience of magic but me (except Joel, who was locked up; and Barb, maybe, but she was too furious to ever speak to me again so it didn't matter).

Lennie had never seen a duel between sorcerers that ended with one of them turned into dry paint, or a rogue wizard sinking in an oily pool of his own evil plans, or for that matter a gallant hero dying in the muddy wreckage of the monster he had just killed. I had.

The others would react like Lennie, recoiling from what had to be done. I even recoiled myself. I felt like the bad guy. It was a repulsive feeling.

Well, what if somebody on the committee really did come up with a better idea, how would I feel about that? If it came from Tamsin, for instance?

Bosanka and Michael had apparently finished. Michael got his book bag and walked away whistling, and something in me died a quiet little death that I almost didn't notice. If the Divine Michael could spend time with Bosanka and not feel anything of the menace of the girl, well, how divine was he?

Bosanka sat on the edge of the stage ignoring us. A man in a trench coat strode past swinging his briefcase and listening to his headset. The guy with the push broom had left.

Bosanka didn't have a coat on, just that thick sweater she wore all the time. Her lips looked blue. More toughening-up for leadership, that was all. I wasn't falling for her facade anymore. I couldn't afford to.

We walked toward her.

"So?" she said.

Lennie grabbed my hand.

I cleared my throat. "We have to talk, Bosanka, honestly. We want to help, but there are some problems."

"Problems," she said, looking north toward the Bethesda Fountain and the rowboat lake beyond. The sculpture angel on top of the fountain ignored us all, observing its own feet as usual.

I said, "Lennie and I are all set to go, and Lennie's sister

Tam, and Peter, I'm sure, when you—when he comes back. That's four of the original committee, which is not bad."

"But," she spat. "I hear 'but' coming. Why should I listen to 'but, but, but'? I want to hear *yes*. I want to hear, we are ready, tell us what to do, make this show on the road!"

"You already know part of the trouble," I said. "We told you. Beth Stowers is in Ohio. There's no way we can get her back."

Bosanka's lips tightened.

"Also, Mimi is gone," I said doggedly, "the girl with the, uh, little mustache, and a mole on her cheek?"

Bosanka looked blank—good grief, did we all look alike to her?—then nodded. "She ran," she said indifferently. "She runs still, but not far. On Saturday she will come, more willing this time."

Lennie said, "She is okay, isn't she?"

"Of course," Bosanka said. She studied her fingernails, which I saw with surprise she had covered with purple polish. "She is needed, like the stupid Peter-boy, so I keep harm away. But this Beth—"

"For Beth," I said as firmly as I dared, "we want to substitute my friend Barbara."

"The black one," Bosanka said, curling her lip.

"That's right," I said, "the black one." The important thing was not to blow up.

She set her jaw stubbornly and looked over our heads.

"Bosanka, come on," I coaxed. "Do we need a whole committee or don't we?"

"What else, 'but'?" she said harshly.

"Joel," I squeaked. "Joel is stuck in Boston."

"So, bring unstuck."

I tucked both my hands in my pockets because they were turning into fists. "I can't, not right away—not by tomorrow! Maybe you can. You're the one who's in charge around here." I was not doing this very well, maybe because I wanted to punch her out.

She said, "You get him."

Lennie said, "Val tried. She went to Boston. You have to help."

"Don't tell me what to do!" she yelled.

I yelled back, "Well, quit throwing tantrums like a little kid who has to be told what to do, then!"

She actually bared her teeth at us. "You are so stubborn against me! Like enemies."

"Jeez," I said, stomping around in a little circle of fury in front of the band-shell stage, "anybody would be against you, the way you behave! This is a free country, you know what that means? We don't do royalty here, okay? Whatever you were at home, around here you're just a scruffy tenth grader, like the rest of us! You have to bend a little bit, Bosanka, or you aren't going to get anywhere!"

"Oh," she burst out, "takes so long, everything here! Everything stands against me! Everything says 'won't,' 'won't,' 'won't,' in not my language! No one is by me to speak my heart's language, saying yes!"

She sat there glaring at us with tears tracking down her cheeks. I was shocked speechless. Bosanka, crying?

Lennie said, "Hey, look, Bosanka—"

"Not my name!" She banged her fist on the edge of the stage. "My people don't know this stupid name, Bosanka!"

Lennie rubbed his forehead as if massaging the thoughts in there, a gesture that made people think he was slow. Sometimes it disarmed them. I'd never seen him use it deliberately before.

He said, "Seven is the magic number, right? On New Year's, the committee was seven, counting Joel. So even if Peter and Mimi are okay and, um, available, what can we do without Joel or Barb? We'd still only be five. We need more time to arrange things so we can all be there. Tomorrow is too soon."

She pointed at him. "*You* don't worry, okay? You think I leave to you, I trust to you? You leave to me. When I need you, I get you. Where I need you, there you go, and what has to do, you will do it for me. Tomorrow, in the night when your moon goes high, you find my people!" She threw back her lank blond hair with a sharp, dismissive gesture. "Go away," she said. "I don't like your foolish faces, your eyes shining false."

"Fine," I said. "We're going."

Outside the park, I stopped at a phone booth and tried to call Barb at home. No answer. I was relieved. I would have to do some fast and furious talking if I did contact her in time, and I wasn't sure I was up to that right now.

When my change came jingling down the return slot, Lennie borrowed some and made a call of his own. I walked around, swinging my book bag, watching my breath frost in the air and wondering what the world would look like under the rule of Bosanka and her "people."

Like a foggy forest full of leaf-takers who had once been people, maybe? And trees that screamed when you hit them if you happened to be in a bad temper that day?

Lennie came and put his hands on my shoulders. He looked mournfully into my face.

"Brace yourself," he said. "Tamsin's gone, too. She took the train to Connecticut to stay with an old friend of my father's so she can attend a dance recital there tomorrow evening. She's not due back until Sunday morning."

"Oh, no," I said hollowly. "That does it, doesn't it? No committee."

"I'll phone up there tonight and try to persuade her to come back," he said, but without real hope. "Hey, I'm sorry.

She's always been—you know—she goes her own way, that's how she is."

"I'm sorry, too. I'm sorry I couldn't hold things together better," I said. Team captain, yeah.

"*We* couldn't," Lennie said. "I told you, you're not hanging out there alone on this—not that the company you're in has done you much good so far."

We sort of leaned our foreheads together and looked down at the space between our feet. I felt so tired, as if Lennie had to hold me up or I'd just drop.

"Listen," he said huskily, "I'm going to take off now—I want to go swim at the Y. Swim and think. Are you okay going home on your own, Val?"

"Fine," I said. "Call me later, will you?"

He brushed my cheek with his mouth, and we ended up kind of wrapped around each other. We had been through the wringer together with more to come, so I guess it's not surprising.

The surprising part was the kiss. It was a real kiss, with us jammed together from our noses to our knees. When we unjammed, Lennie gave me this wild look and said something I don't remember (his voice cracked in the middle of it, I remember that) and loped away. I stood there saying, "Oh boy, oh boy, what was *that*?"

It was not going to the movies and half kissing, half fighting to keep a boy off your entire body. In my limited experience dating always seemed to end up as a wrestling match with a person I didn't know if I even liked, let alone wanted to let anywhere near my physical self.

This was different. This was the kind of kiss you think about when you think about kissing—about how it should be. With somebody who matters to you. It left me feeling dazed but enlightened: so that's why people do it!

What a thing to find out the day before doomsday.

The Patchwork Fiddle, but I'm sorry, that wasn't he, and I...
how should I...

"I'm sorry then. I'm sorry. I couldn't help those feeling.
Never," and then hung up...

13

The Patchwork Fiddle

Mom was setting out ashtrays in the living room, which meant she expected Manley the author. She only put out ashtrays for Manley. Everybody else had to put their ashes in their pockets if they insisted on smoking in our house.

I leaned in the doorway and watched her. She looked nervous and happy but tired, and all of a sudden I saw that she wasn't young anymore. It was a shock to realize this. I guess I had just gone on seeing her as I remembered her from earlier, not noticing the changes. I noticed now and I felt a pang of regret, or something. At least, though, I had managed to keep her safely out of my problem with Bosanka. So far, anyway.

She saw me watching her, smiled, and said hesitantly, "Darling, are you all right?"

"I'm fine," I said. "Any calls for me?"

"There was a message on the machine," Mom said,

bustling out to the hall closet to make sure we had a big hanger in there for Manley's heavy coat. "I wrote it down someplace. Tomorrow's Saturday; how about coming with me to Banana Republic? There's a shirt in the window that looks nice, for either of us."

I said, "I'm busy tomorrow."

She headed for the kitchen. "We're out of cheese again. Think you could pick up a wedge of Jarlsberg somewhere in the middle of being busy?"

It was creepy. Did the smell of danger leak right through my silver wish? She was trying to divert me from my course of doom without even realizing why.

What kind of mom did Bosanka have? Now there was a weird thought. I shook it out of my mind.

"What about my message?" I said.

"Oh, is it important?" Mom said absently, looking over the bottles on the wine shelf.

"For Pete's sake," I yelled, "of course it's important! Isn't it important when somebody calls and leaves a message for you?"

"That depends," she said in the sarcastic tone that meant she was getting ticked off, "on whether the phone is free for a call of mine to get through in the first place. What are you so uptight about? What happened to TGIF?"

"Mom," I said. "My message. What was it?"

She gazed at the ceiling. "Abraham Wechsler called from Boston. He wants you to call him back if you've seen Joel today."

"Seen Joel?" My mouth dropped open. "Seen him where? Joel's in a nuthouse up there!"

Mom checked the ice-cube trays in the freezer compartment. "Mmmm, I had a call from Joel's mother about that this morning. You didn't tell me that the boy had committed himself! Apparently now he's changed his mind. According to his uncle's phone message, Joel has eloped."

"He's *what*?" I screeched.

My God. Not that frizzy-haired girl who'd been sitting on the floor in the TV room! And us with Bosanka and her "people" on our hands! Was Joel really crazy after all?

"It's just a term, Valli," Mom said, standing back for a critical look at the glasses she'd set out on the counter. "It doesn't mean he's run off to get married, just that he's flown the coop. He escaped from the Minuteman Center and they don't know where he is. Now how about a bite to eat, like two civilized people?"

We had sandwiches while Mom talked about Manley and his book and his career and what a talented, wonderful writer he was. I suppose I answered. What I was really doing was listening for the phone and willing it to ring.

Lennie probably hadn't even tried reaching Tamsin yet. I pictured him churning through the Y pool. The waiting was hard—my waiting, Mom's waiting. Her mooning about Manley didn't help.

Manley was a published author. I was just me, and now the stories I had lovingly crafted or sketched out or made notes for would never get into print, except maybe posthumously.

Maybe none of them were any good, anyway. What with the PSATs and finals and so on, I hadn't touched any of that stuff in months, except for the loony-bin story, and we know where that ended up when I reread it after visiting Joel in Boston. Maybe I was going to have my mortal coil shuffled off for me without leaving anything worthwhile behind me, anything my mom could point to afterward and say, "Val did that."

The more Mom extolled the virtues of old Manley, the more my gloom deepened. At one point I believe I said that I thought Manley was about as suited to writing fiction as any ordinary baboon would be if you gave him a word processor to play with. At any rate, Mom was clearly not a bit sad when I chose to absent myself from the scene rather than sit there going crazy.

How in the world was I going to stand a whole day of this tomorrow, until the moon went "high" enough for Bosanka?

I went out and walked through the cold night air to Central Park, crossed the bridle path, and trudged up the hill to Castle Lake. There was the Delacorte Theater, there was the little castle on top of its modest cliff. On the big field north of the lake a monster and my friend Paavo the wizard had died locked in mortal combat, one night last spring. How could the place look so innocent and peaceful now?

My senses felt as if they'd been cranked up high. I heard every whisper of branches and smelled every smell and saw bright, hard edges around everything.

The rush of traffic sounded far away. On my right the lake mirrored the dull glow of the overcast night sky. On my left the meadow stretched wide and empty. Pale cement pathways wound away into the dark among the isolated lampposts. Except for the glow of the widely spaced lamps, it was pretty dark.

It's nighttime and I shouldn't be out here, I thought, but I am and I don't care. This place is magic and it's *mine*, I thought. Damn it, I earned it.

A pinpoint of fire flared and disappeared again immediately, at the east end of the lake under the statue of King Jagiello. Someone was down there smoking a cigarette.

My body went all watery-weak and my feet felt rooted.

Paavo Latvela had smoked—a bad habit he kept, he'd said, to remind himself what it was like to have one. And because he liked it. My heart swelled up with longing. Suppose that was Paavo, come back to help me?

Oh, if only!

The longing passed and I felt quiet and sad. Whoever was having a smoke in the dark down by the statue, it wouldn't be Paavo because Paavo was dead. But who else was fearless and foolhardy enough to hang out here at night, besides me?

I walked softly, on the grass, down toward the end of the lake to have a peek. The smoker cocked his head to blow smoke at the sky, and lamplight fell on his thin face.

Shock jolted me. I marched up to him. "Joel!" I said. "What are you doing here?"

"Smoking." He took another puff.

I noticed the way he held the cigarette, tucked well down between his fingers the way Paavo used to hold his— but I didn't think it would be tactful to say anything. I felt a sudden ache for Joel. He had loved Paavo too.

"Are they after you?" I said. "Are you hiding out here from the Minuteman Center people?"

He shook his head. "Turns out that if you just take off on your own, that's it. Their position is that they did their best to protect you. If you're crazy enough to refuse their protection by actually leaving the premises against their best efforts, legally they're off the hook and good riddance, as far as they're concerned."

"Terrific," I said. "So how did you get down here from Boston so fast?"

"My aunt called her lawyer, after she found me raiding her refrigerator, and he told her all of the above. Since I was home free anyway, she lent me the fare to fly down."

Joel had a thin dark coat on over his sweatshirt and jeans. Didn't he ever feel the cold, for Pete's sake? He did look very tired, though.

"I'm glad to see you," I said, and I meant it, though I wasn't sure whether the Comet Committee's chances were better now or not. With Tamsin in Connecticut and Barb too insulted to join us, we would still be only five out of seven.

"You are?" he said with a nervous laugh. "Don't be too sure."

"What does that mean?" I said. I sat down on the low stone wall that frames Jagiello's terrace.

Joel was quiet, thinking. Then he said, "Remember the day you and I heard Paavo playing music here on this terrace? He drew us like a pied piper."

"Sure I remember," I said. "I think about him a lot." Lately, anyway.

Joel said, "He was a master. He could have taught me to be one, too, if anybody could."

"How are your hands?"

"Rotten," he said.

"Hell," I said. "If only Bosanka was a reasonable person, I'd ask her to help you. It wouldn't hurt her to try to use her magic for something good, for a change."

He shook his head impatiently. "She's no use to me."

"You haven't even met her," I objected, thinking, Some people have all the luck.

"I don't have to meet her," he said. "This is nothing to do with her. It's between me and—somebody else, somebody much older and wiser." He began pacing up and down. "How did I get into this mess, anyway? I always thought music was a way I could live without going nuts."

"I'm sorry about your hands," I said, thinking, older and wiser? That sure wasn't me, so who was it? I could think of one likely candidate, but I didn't know how to ask tactfully about Joel and Paavo Latvela.

"I know what's wrong with my hands," Joel said abruptly. "I've known since it happened."

"That's not what you told me at the coffee shop." I

began to quiver inside. Oh, oh, here it comes, the straw that breaks the camel's back. My back.

"You're so upright, Val," he said, squinting sidelong at me. Smoke streamed out of his mouth. He coughed and lifted his shoulders. "I didn't want to tell you."

Upright? Meaning self-righteous, square? "You still haven't told me," I said.

He mashed the cigarette on the stone wall and flicked the butt out into the darkness. "Think back," he said, "to when those three thugs jumped us here while we were doing magic with Paavo. To the one time you thought I was brave, as you told me up in Boston. Remember what happened right afterward?"

Of course I remembered: Paavo, old and sad, gently putting the broken pieces of his magic violin into the case and kneeling stiffly to sink the case into the shallow waters of the lake—

I leaped up, my heart pounding. "You didn't! Joel, you didn't sneak out here and—and—"

The term that came to mind was "grave robbing," but it was too silly to utter, under the circumstances.

Joel stared past me at the lake. "He sank it right there in front of us for a reason, Val. He wanted us to know where it was. He wanted me to know."

Well, of course—this was Joel, who would do anything to get what he wanted in terms of his musical career. This was what he had been hiding from me, right from when he'd first come to me hoping that my Gran could help him. He just hadn't bothered to fill me in on exactly what he'd done to spoil his hands in the first place, which was to mess with Paavo's magic!

"But how?" I asked, totally bewildered. "That violin was smashed to bits!"

Joel bent and picked up something I hadn't noticed,

something he'd left propped in the shadows at the foot of the wall: a violin case.

"The wood was in good shape," he said, kneeling to open the catches. "The water hadn't affected it all. Of course there was no way to restore the original instrument. I knew that when I took the pieces to the man who works on my father's instruments. What this guy did for me was to rebuild an old fiddle of mine, using parts of Paavo's broken one—the neck, the bridge, and parts here and there."

He stroked the shining wood with his fingertips.

"Joel, you are crazy!" I said. "That's not Paavo's fiddle at all, any more than this statue is the real statue of Jagiello, which the kraken destroyed! They put up a new version of the statue, but it's not the same, and this violin's not the same, either."

"It's close enough," he said softly.

"You mean it works?" I said. "*You tried to play it?*"

"Oh, Val. That was the whole point." He let his spine sag back against the marble plinth of the statue, his elbows on his knees and his hands hanging. "It was ready at the end of the summer. Well, you know what happened. You can figure it out for yourself."

"My guess," I said, "is that that's when your hands went bad on you." I hunkered down facing him and hit him on the leg with my fist. "Damn you, Joel, why didn't you let me in on this? You shouldn't have tried to use Paavo's magic without me! He was my friend before you ever met him!"

That made him sit up all right. "So what? You think nothing can happen without you?" he demanded indignantly. "Anyway, you never would have agreed and you know it. You still don't understand. I wanted something for myself."

The reconstructed violin lay between us, gleaming faintly in its dark, plush bed. Joel's big secret was out at last. No wonder he'd been so skittish when I'd first tried to tell him about Bosanka! He'd been dabbling in magic himself with disastrous results, so naturally he shied away from any more of the stuff, especially since it came in the threatening form of Bosanka Lonat.

"Joel, you dope," I said. "You have to be trained to use magic. I've learned a little from my Gran, but I don't know what I'm doing half the time. I'm not exactly on top of things at the moment, in case you hadn't noticed. Did you really think you were so brilliant that you could pick up where Paavo left off just by playing his violin?"

"I hoped the violin would teach me," he said. "*Something* has to teach me!"

"I don't believe this," I said. "You thought this thing, this Frankenstein-monster of an instrument would turn you into what, some kind of performing genius overnight? And that would show your family and your brother the conductor and—everybody!"

"Oh, what do you know about it?" he said hotly. "Magic, yeah, okay, but music? You don't know beans. As a performer you either have it in a big way or you don't. With this instrument, I thought maybe I had a chance, at least. Sounds pretty selfish, right? Well, talent does that to you. Maybe a little talent does it worse than a lot."

I was horrified. Had he really done some Joel-version of selling his soul to the Devil so he could get a big hand at Carnegie Hall? You just looked at Joel and you could see he was worth more than that, with music or without it! God, didn't he know anything about himself?

I hit him again, harder. He muttered, "Quit that," and tucked his legs further back away from me.

"I don't believe that's the whole reason you took such a totally crazy chance!" I said. "Come on, Joel, talk to me!"

"Valentine, you have only to ask. I have no secrets from you." He sat back and stared straight at me. "I was hoping for power, if you want to know. Not just music but magic, the real thing—the power to change things and make them better. I wanted to heal up the world a little, turn people's minds around so we can maybe make some kind of future for ourselves on this poor, beat-up planet. So I tried to use Paavo's magic. I had to try. I'd even give up music, regular music, to be able to do that."

He held out his hands, flexing his fingers. "Maybe I gave it up for nothing at all. I played this instrument and what happened? My hands quit. I don't even dare try to use the fiddle to help you with your witch-girl because who knows what the damn thing might do to me this time? Or to you? So I didn't make anything better. I made it all worse."

In daylight he would never have said that, and maybe it wouldn't have gotten to me if he had. But it wasn't daylight, and I could tell that he was at the end of his rope.

I hugged him. We ended up huddled together against the cold marble plinth.

"It made sounds," he said into my neck. "I played it out on Boston Common at dawn, and I heard these strange noises—weird yawps and squeals—it was awful. People stared, the few of them there at that hour. There was a guy with his dog, this Great Dane that started barking like mortar fire. A girl actually bolted out of the park holding her head with both hands, it was that bad.

"I remember thinking, it's my bow, I need a magic bow, too. But I knew it wasn't that. So I put the fiddle back in the case and I slunk back to my aunt's place with it, and I haven't played it since. I look at the thing every day, but I'm afraid of it. And I can't play anything else because my hands won't let me."

"You jerk," I said, snuffling into his ear. He smelled of soap and smoke. "Joel, you incredible *idiot*!"

He groaned. "Am I doomed, Val, or what?"

"Probably," I said, backing off a little to wipe my nose. "God, when you want something you really want it, don't you? When I think of you sticking your hands into that dirty water—"

"I wanted to make a difference," he said in a desolate voice.

I said, "That's what everybody wants."

"Shh. Listen." The bushes rustled like rain. Joel craned his neck and said sharply, "Who's there?"

No answer.

A branch lay where it had dropped from the trees overhead. Joel grabbed up the stick and flung it into the bushes.

Two figures crashed out and raced away from us, careering madly along the steep south bank of the lake and pounding up and over the ridge out of sight.

Joel stared after them. "*Two* deer?"

"Peter," I said, "and Mimi, of course!" I couldn't help it, I laughed, a little wildly.

Joel was here, Mimi was tearing through the park with Peter, but we had no Tamsin. I felt like an incompetent sheepdog, rounding up two but losing a third member of my wandering flock. But if Lennie could just get hold of his sister and I could reach Barb, we might still have a chance.

I said, "What are you doing out here by the lake in the middle of the night, anyway?"

What I wanted to hear was that he'd come to try to help us however he could. But when I heard the words out of my own mouth, I thought, Oh no, *the lake*—not that it would be easy to drown yourself in a few feet of dirty water. But this was Joel, remember; Joel in extremis.

He didn't answer right away. I swear I could feel him considering letting me think that he had come to the park to end it all—Joel of the poetic profile and sensitive feelings, oh, what a dreadful pity, etc., etc.

To his credit (though just barely) he decided against self-dramatization and said instead, rather humbly in fact, "Well, my parents aren't home and I was lonesome, and this is a special place, isn't it?"

It was, and it had done some kind of magic for us again. "Come on," I said, "you're coming home with me."

14
Power Lines

Mom was having a drink in the living room with Manley when we got back.

She said, "Hello, darling—oh, hello there."

"Did Lennie call?" I asked.

Mom said he hadn't. "This is Joel, isn't it? I don't think we've ever actually met, have we? Manley, this is Joel Wechsler, a friend of Val's."

Manley shook hands with Joel, who went into his aloof mode. "And what's your métier, young man?" said Manley. He asked this question of a boy standing in front of him holding a violin case, mind you.

"Mental illness," Joel said politely.

Mom slopped some kir on her knee.

Manley wasn't really brain damaged, just tied up inside his own head most of the time, which seemed to interfere with observation of the outside world. To give credit where it's due, he laughed and said, "Well, I guess somebody's got to do it."

I explained to Mom that Joel was more or less in the clear now that he'd liberated himself from the Minuteman Center. She, changing the subject with awesome adroitness, talked with Joel about music—flirting with him, if you can believe that! My incurable mom. For once I was grateful for the existence of old Manley.

Mom said she had played the piano when she was a girl. "I was never much good," she admitted. "I hated to practice."

"You didn't have the right parents," Joel said, gallantly managing not to appear bored. "It takes total tyrants."

"At the risk of seeming like one of those myself," Mom said, looking at her watch, "I'd like to point out that it's getting awfully late."

I said, "Joel and I have some stuff to talk about, Mom. It's important."

We escaped into my room and shut the door.

"Where'd your mom find the Ernest Hemingway clone?" Joel said.

"Hey, the pickings are pretty slim out there," I said. "Anyway, Manley's a lot less awful than some, believe me."

Joel yawned. "I believe you, I believe you." He flopped down on my bed, hugging the violin case, and promptly fell asleep.

I called Lennie's number. Tamsin answered.

"You're back!" I said, feeling my brain clank into some kind of manic high gear.

"Who is this?" Tamsin said.

"It's Val."

"Oh, hi," she said, as in, "Drop dead."

"Tamsin," I said, "I don't know why you changed your mind about running out on us—"

"The dance recital was canceled," she interrupted icily. "And I was planning on coming back tomorrow, anyway."

"Fine, great," I said, "I kiss your toe shoes in apology, okay? This is great! Is Lennie there?"

"No, he's swimming or something. You want to talk to me, or not?" She knew how to throw down the tutu, all right.

"Yes," I said. "Did Lennie have a chance to fill you in on things?"

"He told me some wild story about your wicked witchlet getting all upset with you today, yes. She beat up on a chair?"

"More or less." I wasn't going to explain; let her figure it out for herself, she was so smart. "When he comes back, you can fill *him* in: Mimi's okay, she's in the park with Peter."

"Not Mimi but Bambi?" Tamsin giggled in spite of herself.

"You got it. And Joel broke out of the Boston bin. He's with me."

"Oh," she said, distinctly interested.

I looked over at Joel, sprawled out on my quilted bedspread with his bare ankles gleaming palely between his sneakers and his jeans. I couldn't resist adding, "Well, almost with me. He's conked out."

Tamsin sighed. "I think men look so romantic when they're asleep. Vulnerable, you know? How old is he?"

"Seventeen."

"I thought he was older," Tamsin said, "but of course artistic people are always more mature."

In a pig's armpit. Who the heck did she think she was, talking about "artistic people," her with her lumpy feet and her dippy "attitudes"? She certainly didn't know one single thing about Joel. Except of course that he could be incredibly rude, which some girls find attractive. I've never heard bad manners called "mature" before.

Probably she believed all that crap about how talented people are not only allowed to behave worse than chimpanzees, but are required to behave that way as part of their talent. One good thing, though: She wasn't likely to take off again. She'd stick around if only to see Joel.

"Here's the deal," I said, amazed at the sparks of hope and excitement going off in my exhausted head. "We're all available now, assuming Bosanka can bring the two deer and assuming Barb will come. Bosanka says she'll send for us when she's ready. Well, now we're ready for her! We'll make a comet that will scorch her socks off."

Tamsin said, "Lennie told me your new plan. I think it stinks. It's negative, like black magic, which is always bad, bad news for *everybody* involved."

"Maybe you haven't noticed," I said, "but Bosanka is a witch. We're fighting fire with fire, that's all."

"My spiritual teacher told me," she said, "before the immigration people harassed him out of the country, that black magic turns back against you."

"Great," I said. Who did Tamsin think she was, my Gran? "If you can find your teacher, bring him along tomorrow and he can fix things with Bosanka."

"Don't do a trip on me, Valentine."

"There's no time for a trip," I said. "I've got to call Barbara Wilson. She's on the committee now, too."

"Poor her," she said.

We both hung up.

Joel, the faker, hiked up on one elbow and smiled. "Yes, I really am seventeen and I would like to kiss you," he said. "I mean really, not like on New Year's Eve."

Him, too? Was I putting out some kind of irresistible pheromones all of a sudden?

Was *he*? His clothes were rumpled, his hair was long and messy, his eyes were red, and he was handsomer than

144

he'd been when we had lunch at the coffee shop at the beginning of all this.

Well, the beginning as far as *I* was concerned. Let's remember, this was the person who had resuscitated Paavo Latvela's magic violin months ago and not told me about it until tonight. He was handsome and he was a sneak.

I said, "Forget it, Joel. I'm not exactly in the mood, you know? Where are you going to sleep tonight?"

Not the best question I could have asked at that moment. But out it popped, and I felt my face turn bright red.

"How about right here?" he said, pressing his slightly stubbly cheek down on the quilt and giving me a slow blink, mock sexy but not completely mock, if you know what I mean. "We'll put the violin between us to keep us chaste, like Tristan's sword between him and Isolde."

"No thanks," I said lamely, trying to remember the story of Tristan and Isolde from our mythology unit. Also, my confused feelings seemed to be interfering with my normal eloquence.

Daydreams are one thing. But when the boy is actually right there—I mean, what would it be like to lie down in the familiarity of my own bed, in my own room, with Joel? I did at that moment think fleetingly of Beth Stowers from eleventh grade. What she'd done was beginning to seem just as dumb but not quite so *weird*. I was getting an inkling.

To my huge relief, plus a twinge of disappointment, Joel changed the subject. "I like your room, but it is yours, I don't mean to just barge in and occupy it like an invading army. Can I sack out on that couch in the living room?"

"Fine," I said promptly. "But let's give Manley a chance to leave first."

Joel settled back with his hands behind his head. "So tomorrow is B day, right? And we're supposed to zap her with our mighty powers, whatever they may be and however we do that. Do you think that's what Paavo would do?"

"How should I know?" I said, "He's not around to ask, so we just have to do what we think might work, okay?"

He blinked. "I just wondered."

I sat down on the end of the bed. "Joel," I said, "I can't think of anything else."

"You're doing fine," he said seriously. "You know, now that I think of it, it was an honor to be rescued from the kraken by you. I was just too stupid to know it at the time."

I said, "You sure were, but actually I didn't do it. Not by myself. Gran and Paavo did it, really."

He yawned. "Don't put yourself down. The Comet Committee only amounts to anything at all because you're on it, and if those kids—if we all survive this Bosanka person, that'll be because of you, too.

"The thing is—" He looked troubled. "I'm not sure *I* belong. I want to, it's not that I'm trying to weasel out or anything. But I wasn't on the roof with you on New Year's, whatever anybody says. I wasn't part of whatever you did up there."

"You would have been," I said, "except that you walked out."

He flung himself back against my pillows. "Sure I did! It looked like a seance with a bunch of flakes. How was I supposed to know that anything was really going to happen?"

"You could have stuck around to find out," I said.

"Valentine, that's what I'm saying. My God, am I supposed to spend my entire life apologizing to you?"

It certainly wasn't the first time, he was right about that. But I restrained myself from pointing out that if he'd quit behaving like a spoiled brat, he would also stop providing the occasions for all those apologies.

"Bosanka says you're in the committee," I said, "and I

146

think she's right. You're involved, Joel. Magical stuff of mine has been connected to you from the beginning. You were there when Paavo did magic by the lake. You were part of it, with me. And you're here now, for this. Whatever it is. That's not an accident."

He said wistfully, "Sometimes I catch myself wondering if it ever really happened: Paavo, the Princes of Darkness, the kraken."

"Wait till you meet Bosanka," I said. "If she can happen, anything can."

"So," he said with a big sigh, "should I bring this with me to the committee meeting tomorrow?" He patted the violin case.

"I'm not sure," I said. "Better not. We don't know how to use it, but it might still have some kind of magic, and I'd hate for *her* to get her hands on it."

"Over my dead body," Joel said.

The phone rang. I grabbed it. Barb's voice said, "Valentine? I got something to show you."

Barb sounded excited, not mad. She sounded like her old self again. "Where are you?" I asked.

"In my darkroom."

"I'm there," I said and hung up. I grabbed my coat. "Come on, Joel. Got some money? We need a cab."

As we dashed out I called to Mom from the front hall, "I'm just going downstairs with Joel, be right back."

She yelled something after me, but we were already at the elevator.

"Where'd you leave the violin?" I said.

Joel grinned. "I stashed it under your bed."

Barb lived with her mom and her juvenile delinquent brother in a brownstone on the edge of what I think they used to call Hell's Kitchen. This is probably the last ungentrified chunk of the West Side—below Fifty-ninth, around Eighth and Ninth avenues. I was not unhappy to have a male escort, going down there at night.

Barb generally extolled the area as having the only decent grocery stores and bakeries (mostly Italian, but lots of Oriental places now too) in New York, and other accoutrements of a real neighborhood. Barb has always been gutsier than I am. She's pretty much fearless. I found the place scary.

Barb's apartment is a fourth-floor walk-up with halls the color of dried mucus and stairs that list heavily to starboard and squeal wildly underfoot.

Barb, having buzzed us in downstairs, shouted through the open apartment door, "In here!" We made our way back through the string of high-ceilinged, shadowy rooms, full of couches and chairs with cushions and rugs all over them. Barb's mom has a thing for textiles.

I hollered, "Where's your mom?"

"Cosmetics show," Barb yelled back, "at the Coliseum. Come look at this, you're not going to believe it."

We reached our goal, the tiny back-bathroom which is Barb's bathroom and her darkroom. Barb stood in the glow of the red bulb she'd installed, washing prints in a yellow plastic tray in the sink. Water swished through some kind of siphon arrangement to run off into the topless toilet tank. She had a long apron on over a knee-length T-shirt and ragg wool socks.

"Who's that?" she said, spotting Joel over my shoulder.

"Joel Wechsler," I said.

Barb whispered, "You could have warned me, Valentine!"

She was very sensitive about her legs being skinny, which they were. But right now she was too intent to make more than a token fuss over being caught in a state of massive undress.

"Look at that!" She pointed with yellow plastic tongs at

the print she was rinsing in the tray jammed into the little sink.

There stood Bosanka, holding the wooden dowel like a sword. The oak chair was actually bent, cringing away from her on curving legs. Odd shadowy patterns centering on Bosanka entangled the feet of the chair—curves and lines like faults in the film or the camera lens. Looking closely, I could see actual designs on the stage, around Bosanka and behind her. They showed right through her as if she were transparent.

Stones in a little heap. A row of pennies. A circle of what looked like moulted pigeon feathers. Pieces of glass curved into a spiral. Leaves.

I said, "Barb, what is this?"

"Power," Barb said. "Or an attempt at power, anyway. Look, she's from someplace where they ran things with magic, not fancy technology like ours. She's trying to get a handle on us the way she knows best, with the power patterns she remembers from her home place."

"You're kidding," I said. "I didn't see anything like that in the auditorium this afternoon!"

"Neither did I," Barb said, "but my camera saw it. And that's not all. This is one I took later on. I snuck back in and there was nothing to see, but I snapped a few frames anyway to get evidence, you know, of the broken chair. But look what shows up in the picture!"

She rinsed off a print in which Bosanka didn't appear at all. There was the auditorium stage, and laid out flat on it was a wide triangle of sticks with mismatched ashtrays at the points (I recognized a glazed green one in the shape of a frog from the principal's office). In each ashtray a little flame burned. Stage left, near the curtain, newspapers had been stacked in overlapping piles to make a kind of platform inside lines of acorns and dark twisty things—roots, maybe.

"You didn't actually see this stuff there?" I said.

"Nope." Barb nudged me. "The camera's showing us the tracks of rituals Bosanka must have done in there earlier. I put that splinter of my hand-mirror inside the Leica. This camera takes pictures of magic now!"

"Bosanka's magic," I said. "God, Barb, this is wonderful! You're—you're the world's first psychic spy!" I squinted at the second picture. "That's a bed on the stage, isn't it? Made of newspapers?"

Barb nodded eagerly. "It's like the auditorium is her cave, see? Her lair. She lays out this stuff at night and then she takes it all up again in the morning, before anybody comes. She's been living in the school, Valentine. Sleeping there, raiding the kitchen for food—why not?"

My scalp crept. "But what are the designs for?"

"Power patterns, to protect her while she sleeps," Barb said in a hushed tone.

Bosanka had tried to make herself a guarded place, a place where she felt secure, wound around with scraps of magic from her old world that she hoped would keep our world at bay while she was off her guard, resting. The idea of Bosanka feeling vulnerable enough to need something like that made me feel vaguely ashamed of myself. She was a person, after all, who was good and scared in a strange place, just as Lennie had said.

"Last one," Barb said, fishing the next print out of the smelly developer with her tongs and putting it in to rinse. "Whew. Look at that."

An off-center shot showed a parade of human-size animals drawn in chalk, marching down one wall of the auditorium: leaf-takers. The scene in the jeans store came rushing back to me—drippy fog and the big, doggy-smelling animal whickering anxiously to itself while it patted and turned the wad of purple leaves between its paws.

There in the auditorium Bosanka had drawn more of these creatures, images from home. Maybe she'd hoped to lure her people to her by picturing plentiful game for them.

If she weren't so dangerous, it would have been pathetic. Heck. It was pathetic anyway.

Barb turned in the cramped space to take down some smaller prints from where they were clothespinned to a wire to dry. "These are some shots I took in the park yesterday on the beginning of the roll. Couldn't figure out what any of it was, but I think now I know."

One picture showed a row of pine twigs planted neatly in the ground like small green plumes, with white pebbles placed carefully between them. In the next shot, a parade of gray sticks had been jammed into some cracks in a low, rounded outcrop of rock. Tied to each stick by a tight binding of colored thread was a feather.

"Barb," I said, "I don't get it."

She held up the first little picture next to one of the auditorium. "Same patterns, see it? Force lines, like iron filings aligned by a magnet, but this time set up in the park."

"Where'd you take that?" I said, pointing at the little print of the sticks in the rock.

"Castle Lake. It's a magic place, right? Bosanka has a nose for magic, so she knows that. She's trying to tap into the local current, put it to work for her."

I handed the pictures out to Joel (the bathroom was just about big enough to hold Barb and me, squashed) and took another look at the blow-ups Barb had pinned up under the smaller prints. I was shivering despite the warmth of the overheated apartment.

"What do they do when they find stuff like this in Barbados, Barb? Break it up?"

"Somebody else's juju? You don't touch it, not unless you know very, very well what you're doing."

"Hey, I think I know that girl," Joel said, holding the pictures under Barb's bedside lamp. He pointed at the image of Bosanka. "When I played Paavo's violin on Boston Common that morning, that's the girl who ran away!"

15

Left With
the Check

I felt myself invaded by this slow, silent explosion of understanding—which, for the moment, I managed to keep to myself. While Barb showed Joel more of her pictures (as she furtively kicked some scattered laundry under her dresser before he could notice it), I collapsed on her water bed to think.

"You okay?" she asked me after a little while.

"Fine," I croaked.

"You don't look fine."

She got some cans of soda from the kitchen. I sipped mine, watching Barb trying not to be too interested in Joel (her boyfriend, Rodney, was the jealous type). I watched Joel letting himself doubt that the girl on Boston Common that morning was also the person we knew as Bosanka Lonat.

As for me, I did something pretty new. I kept, as they say, my own counsel.

Barb's whole attitude had changed. She sparkled like

fireworks. She informed me that she was now looking forward to helping turn the tables on the Grand Wazoo of the KKK when the committee met tomorrow at Bosanka's bidding. In fact, she wouldn't miss it for anything.

"Great," I lied. "You are true blue," which was what we had decided we were years ago when some jerk at school had objected that we couldn't be best friends because one of us was black and one of us was white.

For me there was no more Comet Committee, with Barb or without her. There was just what I'd started out with in ninth grade: Joel and me, magic, and a monster. It was up to Joel and me to handle it, and I had an idea of how to do it, too.

Well, *good*. I was fed up with the stupid committee. I was worn out with negotiations and flare-ups and arguments and all the rest of it. I would take on Bosanka alone if I had to. That way at least I knew it would get done.

The rest of that evening is a blur, though I remember taking a cab home with Joel and using the last of his cash to pay the driver. Joel didn't say much. I wondered what he was thinking, but I didn't want to ask. I wasn't up to an argument.

I didn't sleep much that night. Staring at the ceiling, I rambled around in my memories and my fears.

I thought about Paavo and the remains of the fiddle that he had loaded with so much love and care and magic that it would and could do all kinds of magic things for him. I saw him sadly sinking the broken violin in the lake and I thought about Joel fishing it out, probably in the middle of the night so nobody would see, and then waiting, dreaming and waiting, to try its magic that he hoped would answer to him now.

It had answered, all right. When Bosanka had told us she'd heard a call that brought her here out of her limbo, it was Paavo's fiddle that she'd heard.

She had used that call as her lifeline out of limbo. Rushing to find the source, she must have come skidding to some kind of halt on Boston Common on that late summer dawn. But Joel had stopped playing, leaving her without anything to guide her. Bosanka, overwhelmed by the strangeness of an alien world after all that silence and isolation, had panicked.

Lennie was right, he was always right about stuff like this. She was not invincible, a girl of ice. She'd run away, losing the connection she might have made with Joel and the magic "voice" she'd heard.

Until our Comet Committee connected her up with us, and through me, of course, with Joel. But everything had begun with the use of Paavo's fiddle. Which meant there was a way out. Maybe. An easy but horrible way out.

Joel had, as it were, reconstituted the fiddle from concentrate, and it had called Bosanka. What if we reversed the process? If he broke the instrument down again, if we returned the fragments to their watery grave, maybe that would uncall her and she would vanish back where she'd come from, all her own magic undone as well!

Assuming I could convince Joel, or get the violin away from him (he had insisted on sleeping with it next to him on the couch), and do the job myself.

Suppose I was wrong? Suppose it didn't work?

Suppose Joel responded to my brilliant idea by smashing the magic fiddle over my head?

It was so unfair—Paavo gone, Gran comatose, and *me* stuck with all this.

Saturday morning came, gray and chilly. I got up and had coffee with my mother before she left. One of her authors was in town for a weekend writers' conference and they were going to have a business lunch together. Joel looked like a lump wrapped in a quilt on the living room couch.

Mom, quiet and worried-looking, hunched over her coffee cup and watched me. She wore her faded velour bathrobe that I hoped to inherit someday, it was so soft and drapey and rich-looking. She was like a picture, my mom, slightly removed from the events at hand. Our lives, lived close together in mutual support for so long, had really taken two different paths back when the family talent that she rejected had first tapped me on the shoulder, and I had gone with it into my first magical adventure.

Now maybe I was launched on my last one.

"Sweetie," Mom said. "What's wrong?"

I said, "Something, Mom, but you can't help."

Reaching across the tabletop she took my hand and stroked the back of my knuckles with her thumb. I let her. I even squeezed back a little.

In a sheepish tone she said, "Am I smack in the middle of it acting like a damn fool, like last time? And not even knowing it?"

So she did remember something about having been wooed and almost won by the horrible Dr. Brightner! She had never mentioned that episode since Gran and I had set Mom free from his enchantment.

I said, "Not this time. This time it's definitely me in the middle, and if anybody's acting like a damn fool, that's me too."

"I wish I could help," she said.

"Mom," I said, "if there was anything you could do, believe me, I'd ask."

"You're sure there's nothing?"

I shook my head and got up. "I better go wake Joel," I said. "We'll go down to the coffee shop for breakfast."

I knew Mom would feel easier about leaving the two of us alone in the apartment if we were up and dressed and on our way out of the place. My silver wish would keep her

156

from interfering in any case, but I felt better behaving the way I knew she would have expected if there'd been no silver wish.

I also wanted to be in a public place when I broached the subject of trashing the violin, so Joel would have less scope for dramatics. You don't want to look like a spoiled baby in a coffee shop full of people on their way to attend to the business of the grown-up world.

As it turned out, we all left the apartment together. Joel had the violin case with him because I'd asked him to bring it.

Mom flagged a cab. She pulled my head down and gave me a quick kiss on top, the way she used to when I was a little kid. "If you change your mind," she said, "leave me a message on the answering machine."

She ducked into the cab and zoomed off down West End Avenue.

At the coffee shop I had juice and a chocolate eclair, for energy. Then I told Joel he would have to smash the violin and throw it back in the lake.

He turned pure white. "No," he said, very loud.

"Sshh," I said. "People are staring."

He shoved away his plate of half-eaten omelet and his fork fell on the tile floor with a deafening jangle. Anybody who hadn't been staring before was staring now.

"You can't ask me to do that," he said. "You can't!"

I leaned across the table toward him. "Joel, think a minute! It's our best chance, and if it works, you'll probably be cured at the same time." Two ladies near us had suspended their conversation to listen in, looking nervous. "Your hands, I mean," I added quickly. "If we uncall Bosanka, I bet we fix your hands at the same time. We undo everything in one fell swoop without any of us getting hurt, don't you see?"

157

"*I* get hurt!" he answered. "What about me?"

"It's called taking responsibility for your actions, Joel," I said, sounding a lot tougher than I felt. I knew what that violin meant to him.

"You mean *I* started all this?" he said, holding on to both sides of the table as if that was all that kept him from exploding through the ceiling. "You want to load this entire mess on my shoulders? If Joel will only take it all back like a good little boy, a lot of bad things will just not have happened? It doesn't work that way, Valentine!"

His lips were paler than the tablecloth. I was shocked, dismayed, and fascinated. I'd never thought people looked like that outside of the movies. Could mere words of mine have produced an effect like this?

"Listen, Joel," I pleaded, "you're not being rational. It's not anybody's fault, but you and I are the ones with a real chance to fix things without risking the necks of a bunch of essentially innocent people who just happened to get caught up in all this. Come to the lake with me. Bosanka wants magic when the moon is high, so we'll do it when the sun's at its peak, to make things as opposite as possible: noon. We'll do it together. Paavo was a friend to both of us, he'd understand."

"No," he whispered.

"Joel, what's the difference? You can't play the thing, so what good does it do you to keep it?"

His chair flipped over with a crash. Joel snatched up the violin case and ran out of the restaurant.

"The lake at noon, we've got to try!" I screamed. I would have run after him, but the waiter stopped me. Joel had left me with the check.

By the time I shook off the questions and paid the bill, he was gone. Whether he would come to the park at noon or

t was up to him. There was nothing more I could do. It
emed like I had done more than enough already, and
thing that I did worked out right.

It was still early. I headed for the hospital, feeling
rible and slow, as if I weighed a million tons. They let me
to see Gran even though it was before official visiting
urs. I must have looked totally desperate, which I was.

Gran lay curled on her side with her mouth open and a
mp patch on the pillowcase under her cheek. Nothing that
did made any difference. Not words, not tears, not patting
r hand and kissing her cheek and trying to hug her, which
as the point at which the nurses hustled me out of there
ndly but firmly.

I walked around the city like a zombie. I couldn't rest
ywhere. The Indian restaurant once run by Ushah the
wful had been turned into a doughnut shop. I went to the
tle midtown waterfall park where Paavo had gone to rev up
r his final assault on the kraken. I walked to the sidewalk
ating that had once let me conspire with Joel, the blind
isoner of the phantom subway station.

At the skating rink at Rockefeller Center I stood shiver-
g and watched a huge machine clean the ice. My fingers
oze and my nose dripped and my head echoed with stupid
oughts leading nowhere. At least I had some breakfast in
e to keep me physically alive.

Finally I found myself drifting through the park to
astle Lake, hoping that somehow Joel would relent and
ome to meet me there at noon after all, with the violin.

People were gathered at the east end of the lake, on the
assy edge of Jagiello's terrace: Lennie, and Tamsin wearing
ne of her artsy-fartsy outfits with tights showing off her
gs. Barb was taking pictures with her ancient Leica.

"Where's Joel?" she said when she saw me, and I almost
umpled up right there.

"You look half dead," Lennie said, grabbing me by t arms and peering anxiously into my face. "I tried to call yo Where were you?"

"It's a long story," I said, glancing at Barb. Her face w hidden behind the camera. "What are you all doing here?"

They each said that I had phoned them and asked the to come to the lake at noon for a Comet Committee meetir and what was wrong with me, didn't I remember? I began wonder if I had called them, and had somehow forgott that I did it. Should I tell them about Joel and the patchwo fiddle? I was confused and afraid to tell them anything.

It was getting close to twelve.

Tamsin said, "But we don't have Peter and Mimi he how can we be the Comet Committee? And I mean Peter a Mimi, not a couple of deer."

Tamsin was not sentimental about animals, only abo herself. I found this one of her least endearing characteristic

"They'll turn up," Lennie said, looking confidently arour He had on the same huge tweed coat he'd worn on Ne Year's Eve on the rooftop, and woolen gloves on his hands. wasn't that cold with the sun shining, but Lennie has nev really gotten used to North American winters.

"They'll show," Barb agreed. "Animals are attracted concentrations of psychic energy."

"According to whom?" said Tamsin.

"According to people who know," Barb said, and Tams sniffed but let it go at that.

Animals? I wondered if we were about to be overru with squirrels, which the park is full of. What were we doir here? Everybody looked at me as if I should know, and I w totally at a loss.

Tasmin turned her attention to me, asking like an ech of Barb, "So where's Joel?"

Lennie came to my rescue. "We didn't need Joel on the pot when we first formed the Comet Committee," he said. "Who says we need him now?"

"Bosanka says," Tamsin said, "or so everybody keeps telling me."

"Hey," Barb said. "There he is." She made some quick camera adjustments and began clicking off pictures as Joel strode toward us carrying the violin case.

He walked up in grim silence and set the case down in front of me. "Well," he said, glaring at me, "go ahead. Jump on it, or whatever you have in mind."

I didn't know what to say. I hadn't meant that he should destroy the magic fiddle in front of everybody like this! Just the two of us would be bad enough. He might not believe it, but I knew how he felt. This was Paavo's magic we were talking about.

"Why do you want to break your violin?" Tamsin asked. For the first time she sounded unsure.

Joel stuck his hands in the pockets of his thin coat and stared with bright, red-rimmed eyes around the little circle of us. "I don't want to. Valentine says it has to be done. So who's going to do it? Nobody? All right, then."

He raised his foot over the old black case.

Lennie said, "Hey, wait a minute, is this the one Val told us about? The magic one?"

"It *was* the magic one," Joel said bitterly, and he stomped down.

But he seemed to slip, and I saw his foot land not on the violin case but on a little tepee of gray sticks planted in the soft earth alongside the lake. There were small cracking sounds, and I saw the other little stickpiles collapsing like dominoes, in a line that ran back the way Joel had come.

I saw the other lines, power lines Bosanka must have planted—pinecones behind Lennie, twists of grass behind

161

Barb, stones winking with mica behind Tamsin—and I knew what had brought them all here; not phone calls from me!

Looking back, I spotted the markers that had led me here, too—oak leaves, brown and withered, each pinned to the ground with a thorn. I felt those thorns in my stupid sinking heart.

In the blink of my eyes we were all shut in by a dense white wall of fog. Somewhere beyond the wall, I heard soccer players on the big field hollering in Spanish or Italian, but could only see a few yards ahead.

I could hear dogs, too. They barked, they howled, they were coming closer.

A pack. Bosanka the hunter had assembled a pack.

Joel, kneeling by the violin case, looked up at me with dawning fear.

I nodded, almost too scared to speak. "She's coming," I gasped. "She sent for the committee, just like she told us she would: Joel, we can't let her get her crazy hands on Paavo's violin!"

Joel groaned. Then with one strong sweep of his arm he grabbed the violin case, turned, and slung it into the fog, in the direction of the lake. There was a splash, and a sob from Joel, and then two deer hurtled out of the fog into our midst fleeing from the yelling of the dogs we couldn't yet see.

I caught panic from the deer, and I flailed my arms at the dense white fog and ran.

16

All the Day They Hunted

I ran like water runs down a cliff, throwing myself madly over or around anything that loomed up in my way—a scarred park bench, a tree, a low red picket fence around an eroded slope. A long-legged stag caromed off my side as we sped through an echoing cave, one of the stone tunnels of the park.

I heard others, their steps, their hard breathing, as we raced through the park, skittering over pavement and dry winter grass in perfect, mindless, animal terror.

With the tiny part of my mind that stayed helplessly human, I understood that Peter and Mimi had joined us—we were a whole little herd of running deer. The Comet Committee was meeting, all right, in headlong flight.

We ran deeper into the chilly mist that hung everywhere like soggy laundry stuffed down among the trees. At times I seemed to run all alone and then I would hear distant barking, or the breathing of another running deer somewhere near me in the dimness.

After what felt like a year, the fog began to tear and trail away. Seams of bleak light opened that might have been night or day, I couldn't tell with my black-and-white deer vision. When I stared back over my shoulder (where my own hide was dark with sweat), I saw dogs pouring after me, red tongues lolling gleefully from fanged jaws.

Behind them or among them, Bosanka was like some tireless, horrible monster in a nightmare that you can't shake off your trail. She ran with a steady, easy stride and her face, when I could see it in the gloom, was cold and merciless.

The sight of her filled my animal heart with a pounding terror that drove me even faster.

The fog vanished, the air was dry and still. I longed for the fog again, to dampen my parched throat.

We ran through woodland, hilly and rough. Dead tree branches reached up to catch our legs as we leaped over them. The soil made little dry crunching noises at each step, and plumes of ash were kicked up by our hooves. We crossed wide patches of bare, bruising, rock-hard earth.

Central Park was gone. We were somewhere else, running over an alien land that was dead.

Once we split up, not by plan—we weren't capable of planning—but because the flat broke into spreading hills, like the fingers of a withered hand.

It made no difference. Bosanka harried us one by one.

I hid, gasping for breath, in a gloomy tangle where fallen trees crisscrossed and held each other up. My legs shook, my heaving sides steamed. I strained to track the dogs as they thrashed along somewhere near.

Through my human mind ran the refrain of one of my favorite nursery rhymes from my old Mother Goose book, about three jolly Welshmen who go hunting and don't bag anything but have a dandy time. It went something like this, "And all the day they hunted, and nothing could they find, but a ship a-sailing, a-sailing with the wind."

All the day was a long, long time.

Something came snuffling toward my hiding place, and panic sent me crashing out of my scraggly cover again. I nearly fell over the ribs of a dried-up carcass, a thing like a kangaroo with its jaws open in the dirt—the remains of a leaf-taker. The faint, musty stink of it sent me bounding desperately on.

My lungs were going to explode, my heart would split open and drown me in my own blood. But I ran, and the others ran with me: down through a forest of blackened toothpick-trees and out across an endless marshy flat crusted with dried salt and dotted with jumbled ruins.

Every time we stopped for breath—and she let us do that purposely, I think, to prolong the hunt—we would see her trotting toward us with dogs around her, and we would run again.

It was during one of these rests that I realized I was not just running away. There was a scent in the air that I followed, a moist tang that had to be the smell of water. "Nothing could they find, but a ship a-sailing." It was toward the water-trace in the hot, dead air that I ran, and the others followed me.

At last we moved at a stumbling trot out onto a windy, steep-sided headland. Dead-ended, we stopped, milling sluggishly at the edge of the bluff. There was a gray beach below, littered with bones and seaweed. The sea beyond looked like black glass.

Water—and a dead end.

A young stag banged into me, smearing my neck with foam. My long deer-tongue hung out of my mouth and my throat was cracking with dryness. If I could have reached it, I would have plunged my long face into that dark sea down there and drunk it up.

Bosanka laughed. We shambled around to face her, a trembling group under a high, bright sun.

She stood a little way off in her jeans and sweater and boots with her arms crossed—First Hunter, boss of the forest. I couldn't take my eyes off the dogs, which sat at her feet panting and looking at us. They weren't the red-eyed hellhounds I had imagined chasing us over Bosanka's ruined world but a bunch of grubby Manhattan strays, lop-eared and tangle-coated. One of them was a Pekingese.

My human mind jeered incredulously, she's got me terrified of a *Peke*?

This made a little bubble of laughter deep in my mind somewhere. Right away I felt my deer shape drifting and leaning, as if it were coming loose from an outline that had been drawn to hold it in. I felt shaky and feverish.

If only I could unhitch the last little hooks of my consciousness and float away from the staggering deer-Val before Bosanka let her dogs loose on us!

"Now," she said, "you do what I say. You make your committee, you send your signal of light. Then, if we wish it, my people and me will hunt you together, to the kill."

We all crowded close, leaning on each other—oh, the sound of our lungs laboring, the sharp tang of our terror, the flash of our despairing eyes!

I was the one with the magic grandmother. I was the one the others had all followed here. And I was the one who was not going to be chased another step by Bosanka, her people, and a snuffly little Pekingese.

I turned and made a last-ditch, gallumphing dash for the end of the bluff. There I dug in my hooves and more or less threw myself out over the sea. Falling, I heard the hoofbeats of the others running to leap after me, and—so gratifying—Bosanka's startled shout.

We're dead, I thought as I smashed through a great weight of icy, inky water. I saw stars and began to drown. I had just opened the inevitable crack of acceptance when something drove up from below and booted me rudely to the surface.

I broke through the water gasping and choking, a human being again. Hands grabbed at me, people pulled me bruisingly over the side of a boat. "A ship a-sailing, a-sailing with the wind"—good old Mother Goose! These people who were tugging at me and manhandling me up out of the water swore and gasped and urged each other on in voices that I knew: the Comet Committee.

I flopped down on the wet, chilly bottom of the boat. Nobody paid me any further attention. They were busy hauling somebody else in from the water.

What I had thought with my deer vision to be the sun was in fact the full moon. Bosanka had hunted us through the day to the moonlit Saturday night that she herself had appointed for her meeting of the Comet Committee.

They put the next rescuee further up front in the boat, and then Lennie hove up over the side and nearly fell on me, dripping and blowing and burbling exultantly, "Did you see them? It's dolphins, I can't believe it, they held Barb up in the water until I got to her! God!"

He hugged me hard and I hugged him squelchily back. He was sleek and soaking, like a dolphin himself. "Are you okay, Valentine? You're all right, aren't you?"

I was. It was as if the icy water had washed all through me and flooded out all the aches and exhaustion and despair of the hunt in one shocking rush. My hair and clothes were already drying in a warm breeze that blew out of the clear night sky. I sat up and looked around.

We were in an old wooden boat coated with layers and layers of scarred paint, like the boats you rent at the rowboat lake in Central Park. But we were not in Central Park. We were floating on a wide, moon-sparkling sea. I couldn't see a sign of land, a wink of man-made light, or the shadow of another vessel anywhere.

No one spoke. We coasted quietly up the back of one long swell and down another. The water made small lip-smacking noises around us. Little flips of foam popped off the crests of the swells or curled like lacy fans down their backs. This was deep, open water if ever I saw it, mysterious and beautiful under the moonlight.

Here we were bobbing lazily around in a park rowboat in the middle of the night on what appeared to be something on the order of the Atlantic Ocean.

"Oh my God!" I said. "Where are we?"

Peter croaked, "Look up there. Those are the stars of the southern hemisphere."

I tried to take stock of our situation. I mean, you have to start coping somewhere, no matter how crazy things are, right?

Up on the single seat at the prow of the boat, Joel crouched facing forward, away from the rest of us. Barb hunched in the bottom between him and the next seat down, coughing up water and swearing foully in a choked voice. On the next seat, Peter was trying to explain to Mimi, who sat next to him, how to work the oars to help steady the boat, though we obviously weren't going to row anyplace in particular.

On the widest seat, in front of me, Lennie had settled next to his sister. He craned his neck to see over the sides of the boat, watching for dolphins. Tamsin leaned against him and massaged the muscles of her legs with her hands.

Then there was me, on the bottom. So there we were, the whole Comet Committee, all in the same boat.

And in the stern, gripping the edge of the last seat, was Bosanka Lonat with her ice-chip stare fixed on me.

"Bosanka?" I said stupidly. "What are you doing here?"

"You ask that!" Seawater dripped from her hair, and her teeth chattered audibly even though the night was warm. "You did a trick on me! I have no place here. Hunting the sea is for the Lords of the Waters. You never told that you were one!"

A "Lord of the Water"? Me?

Well, maybe, in a way; the smell of water had drawn me, and water had restored me, and that wasn't all.

There was the violin sunk in the lake that had somehow preserved it; Gran showing me a vision of Joel in a birdbath full of water; the image of Paavo rippling like waves down in the Eighty-first Street subway station; even rotten Dr. Brightner capturing my mother and trying to capture me with ice—*frozen* water. Not to mention the moving water that powered each of my silver wishes—good magic had always been connected with water.

Bosanka was afraid, and she was right to be afraid. We weren't in her foggy forest or her dead world now but on the open sea of good, strong Earth water.

"Now what, you kill me?" she said harshly.

"Don't worry," Peter said. "They'd like to, but nobody's got the guts."

"It's too late," Barb groaned, hunching over her camera, which was hanging from her neck on its strap. "My Leica's ruined, and it's that girl's fault!"

"What's the matter with you people?" Lennie bubbled joyfully. "We've got help here, the best kind of help! Don't you realize we just had our lives saved by dolphins?"

"That thing bumping me in the water?" Bosanka's broad shoulders shrank in a kind of cringe. "Was it 'dolphin'?"

"Had to be," Lennie said happily. "There are stories of them saving drowning people. Where'd they go? Can anybody see them?"

Tamsin grabbed his arm. "Quit leaning out like that, you'll tip us over!"

A little moan of terror escaped from Bosanka. I was not above being delighted to hear it.

Something in the atmosphere began to move, stirring around us like wind. A change was coming. My skin prickled and my blood zinged. This is it, I thought. This is what my silver wish bought for me, the freedom to be here, tonight, for this—whatever it is.

The boat slapped down in a trough of water, and something slid out from under the stern thwart and bumped my leg: a violin case, of course. My heart gave a thump like a war whoop.

Destroy Paavo's violin? Of course not! That was a craven way to go, a baby way. There was a better choice, if we were brave enough. We floated on a sea of good magic now. It was time to trust that magic and its gifts, or die trying.

I said, "Pass this to Joel, it's his."

Without a word they handed the case up to the prow. Joel, turned to face into the boat now, looked at the battered fiddle-case for a long moment before he reached out and accepted it. He set it across his knees, opened the lid and lifted out the violin and bow.

Barb took back the empty case and tucked it somewhere in the bottom of the boat, which except for the water dripping from our clothes was only medium damp. She kept the square of silk that had covered the violin strings, and began tenderly wiping off her camera with it.

I wondered how Joel's hands felt, how his heart felt, but

I kept my mouth shut. This was his moment, not mine. I was glad for him in a fierce way—go for it, Joel!

I had a strong feeling of events inexorably gathering, and of there being, somehow, enough time.

Joel lifted the instrument and tucked its wide end under his jaw. His eyes glinted as he lifted his head slightly, shooting me a defiant look down the length of the boat. I understood that look: he was petrified, but he was ready.

I was, too. "Bosanka," I said, "you asked what we'll do now. We're going to answer your magic with some magic of our own. The call that began your visit here should have the power to end it."

Peter noisily shipped his oar, holding it across his lap like a weapon. "I say we just heave her over the side."

Lennie said, "Can it, Peter. We're way past that, okay?"

"Speak for yourself," Peter said sullenly, but he piped down.

I don't know how much Bosanka understood. She didn't give any sign that she recognized Joel from that dawn on Boston Common, or connected the violin itself with the call she had followed there. What was obvious was that she was terrified of the sea.

She said to herself in a despairing whisper that I think only I heard. "Calm down, junk-boy, you get what you want. This water is my death."

She sat rigid, stoic now, cut off from the powers of her high-forest home and alone with us on our earth's ocean. I didn't know what would happen when Paavo's magic violin in its new incarnation was asked to speak, but I was ready to find out.

"Joel," I said, "will you try to play the violin?"

With a flourish, Joel drew the bow across the untuned strings, using the bow and the fiddle exactly as they had

171

come to him. If I put my trust in the water, he put his in the instrument.

What did I expect? That Paavo would walk to us on the water, or Sorcery Hall appear in the form of a Spanish galleon, or Gran's voice sing a spell to music that would set everything right?

Something. I felt a force rising to meet us already, and it was something grand.

A wild, deep note skirled upward from the fiddle into a staccato squawk, at which point the water all around us erupted in flashing silver arcs.

Lennie shouted, "The dolphins! There are the dolphins!"

The air shivered with sounds too high to hear. Joel played on the edge of silence and over it, past the limits of human hearing, and the great dark backs of whales broke from the water like islands forming without smoke or fire.

17

Water Music

All around us they glistened huge and shining, spurting their noisy breath in pale geysers against the sky.

Bosanka leaped up shrieking, "What is it, what is it?"

I screamed back, "Sit down, sit down, you idiot!"

A shape like a conical mountain heaved up out of the water about twenty feet away. A baseball-size eye gleamed at us from the corner of a mouth like the Grand Canyon turned on end.

Bosanka flopped back down on her seat, lifting her hands defensively. "What is it?" she wailed.

I was too breathless to speak, but I remember thinking with an edge of hysterical humor, Something bigger than a little old leaf-taker, kid.

"Bosanka, it's okay," Lennie said, leaning past me to make urgent gestures of calm, patting the air with his hands. "Don't be scared." Sleepy-eyed, easygoing old Lennie quivered like a hot wire and his eyes glowed. "That's a whale spy-hopping, that's all—sticking his head out of the water to have a look at us."

Tamsin stared openmouthed, hugging her knees. Mimi reached into the water, begging, "Oh, let me pet you, come closer!" Tears sparkled on her cheeks like diamonds.

Another whale surfaced close to the other side of the boat, about ten feet from Peter.

"Awesome," he breathed. "Oh, *look! Awesome!*" He jiggled around on his seat like a small, excited boy.

Barb groaned softly to herself, looking longingly out over the water, her ruined camera clutched in both hands.

I turned back to Bosanka, feeling light-headed with excitement. But my voice came out calm. There was no need to shout over the sounds of the violin.

"The whales are the biggest warm-blooded animals alive on the earth. They're wonders to us. People save up time and money for years to go out in boats just for a chance to see them. Tonight they've come here to us. Why?"

She shook her head wordlessly.

Mimi murmured, "Who cares? Oh, look!"

A formation of dolphins flew past one of the water giants like white birds past a volcano. They vanished in the water with tiny foam splashes. Two of the huge heads slipped quietly back under and others came up. One bunch of dolphins went wheeling away and some others swooped toward us, spraying us with feathery spume as they hit the water.

I began to distinguish other sounds mixed in with the skittering, swooping voice of the violin: beepy, squeaky, boomy noises, in the air and in the water. The thick planking vibrated through my shoe soles.

Bosanka wouldn't or couldn't answer me, but the whales and the dolphins would. If I just waited, if I could just sit quiet and not force things—there was enough *time*, I would understand, I would know what to do or say next. I swallowed the little surges of panic that kept spiking up into my happiness, and I waited.

"Oh," Lennie said suddenly, clapping his hands down on his knees. "Bosanka, it's a message for you. They say they're glad you came. They say it's about time."

Bosanka turned her hopeless glance on him. "What are they to me, these things?"

"They're your people," he said with respect and admiration. He grinned. "You wanted us to find them, and we have."

I laughed, it just broke out of me—so much for Bosanka's plan to take over the earth, if she'd had one! So much for our fears!

"No!" cried Bosanka furiously. "These are monsters!"

Joel whipped a jaggedy yowl out of the violin, with a tremulous whine fading up at the end, out of hearing. I recognized this as a translation of Bosanka's protest into another language, a language of sound and emotion instead of words.

A great burst of clicks and peeps and squawks from the water followed.

Lennie said, "I can't make it out, they're so—" He looked around frantically. "Can anybody—?"

Mimi said, "You don't hear that? I do." She wouldn't look at Bosanka or address her directly. "They say—she still has the kind of body they had on their old world, but these are their new forms, here on this one."

At long last I let go of something I hadn't even known I'd been holding clenched inside me. All I heard was a riotous racket rising from the water all around us, none of which made the slightest sense to me. But it was all right as long as *somebody* understood it. And as long as the whales and dolphins understood whatever translation of our language Joel played in sea-mammal talk, on Paavo's magic violin.

Mimi went on breathlessly. "They say, she's a good hunter to have found them. They hoped she would. On their old world, they were all hunters with great hunting magic. They could draw pictures of their prey and make certain—certain designs, and that would force the prey come to them to be killed, you know, for food—and also later for sport and for, um, like showing off. None of the animals could resist for long.

"So Bosanka's people wiped out some kinds of creatures that—well, without them the whole ecology fell apart. Everything died, including them. Except Bosanka. They sent her off away from all that, with their magic. They sent her on a spirit journey where she'd be safe until they could call her."

Blank-faced, Bosanka looked from one of us to another.

Three dolphins arced past an arm's length away, breathing explosive, sudden breaths when they broke the surface. Then they were gone again, smooth as silk.

"My turn," Tamsin said dreamily. "Oh, it's so spiritual! All their bodies died, and their souls came looking for another world to live in. But they didn't want to be a dominant species anymore, so they opted to live as these great sea mammals, the whales and the dolphins. Not hunters so much as hunted, at the mercy of the earth's dominant species—people."

Bosanka hit her thighs with her fists. "Lies, you all lie! My people are lords of everything, the forest and the sky and all the creatures!"

Joel played hard, twanging notes and got for an answer an uproar in the water.

"That's the point," Tamsin said. "They were all that on their old world, and they did a very lousy job. So they don't

176

want to do it anymore. They've deliberately given up hands, because of what they did when they had them—they abused the power that the works of their hands, their magic arts, gave them.

"They invented all those spells where you set up your stones and your leaves and things, with your hands. The power they called up and directed that way made their world and everything in it do just what they wanted. That was their way of dealing with their world, just like tools and science are our way. That was their power.

"They say they hope that we learn the lessons of power, too, but better and faster so we can keep this world alive, which is more than they did with their own." She grimaced. "They say it doesn't look good, though. They die by the thousands because of the technology our hands have made, and they see lots of other creatures dying, too, because of us and the ways we live. But they try to stay hopeful."

Bosanka shouted out over the crowded water, "I am a highborn, a leader, a power among my own. If you are my people, *why did you leave me?*"

The echoing cry of the violin was painful. Joel played something that made me remember being little and lost at Jones Beach one time, and how it felt to be one lone speck in all that sunny, salty, sandy space, thinking I'd been left because I'd done something wrong.

The outburst of sea voices was softer now, more blended.

Barb cleared her throat. "It's like this," she announced. "They say, 'We left you to follow, to find us, to track us, here to our new life in far-distant seas. We left you to bring us these friends with you, handed-folk, youthful and open, to carry our song home and sing to their own kind the lessons of power.' "

"They hid from me," Bosanka said, "by purpose!" She looked absolutely stricken. I knew now more about how

177

she felt than I had any wish to. Somehow Joel was playing the afternoon when I came home from grade school and Mom sat me down in the living room and said, "Honey, Daddy's not going to be living with us anymore for a while. He's taking a long trip."

In fact he had already gone, and he never came back, and I couldn't figure out what had happened but I knew it had to be because I'd done something so awful that Mom couldn't even talk about it. Even now that I knew it hadn't been my fault at all, just remembering how I'd felt then made my eyes smart.

I heard Bosanka say bitterly, "So, good, they approve that I track them, I find them. Should I die now, go crazy, what?" Joel played the night that Paavo Latvela died, or anyway that's what I heard. Other people in the boat cried over private meanings of their own.

The boat turned lazily in the riot of clicks and hoots and whistles that answered.

Barb spoke like an oracle announcing a decision of the Fates: "Listen. They say, 'The choice you were born for is bright with this moon, join us or leave us, be swimmer or runner, be hand-folk or fin-folk. Our powers are cast off, except for a small part, we saved it for you, child, to alter your form. Your lone swim is over. You drew these young handed-ones here for our speaking, and now this is done. Your questing is over, your worth is well proven. You are our daughter, and we are your people. Land-choice or sea-choice, we love you forever, we sing you forever, you live in our songs.'"

Bosanka, her mouth drawn down like the mouth of a theatrical tragedy mask, blurted out, "I don't come all this way to be—to be *animal!*" She pointed shakily at me. "When we are on land, Balentena, I will kill you for this low magic that turns my people into—into—"

"What is wrong with you?" Barb said fiercely. "They want you! Which is more than you deserve, girl!"

"You don't know, witch of the dark!" Bosanka spat. "This is beasts! I am a highborn, a master, a hunter! I don't want *them*!" She brandished her fists over the water. "Go away, leave me! I, Horn's Breath, First Hunter of the High Forests, the last of my true people, I don't want you!"

"Bosanka, don't!" came Lennie's anguished cry over the howl of the violin.

The sea-people answered.

Peter nudged Lennie's back with his foot. "Leave it, man, it's over. They're going. They're saying good-bye." He paused, looking embarrassed. "I can't do it like, you know, poetry."

"Just say it out," Barb said impatiently, and Mimi said, "Don't worry, Peter, it's not a contest!"

Peter stood up with the easy balance of somebody used to boats. He composed himself and with a sort of formal stiffness recited what he heard the whales and dolphins say.

" 'The choice is your choosing, it saddens us greatly, but our tides still call us'—uh, something about they have maps to make and places to put in their songs still—uh—'We sing the seas' heartbeat, our work spins us onward—' They don't want you to be sad, though they know you will be. 'In dreams you may hear us, singing your choosing, farewell and remember, remember, recall.' " He stopped, bowed a ridiculous little bow, and sat down.

Joel had lowered his bow and the violin at last. His shoulders loosened and his head dropped back a little so that the moon shone on his face. He had done real magic tonight, magic that Paavo himself would have been proud to do. This was Joel's triumph, and he blazed with it.

Nobody could stay like that for long, it would burn them up. But I didn't want to see his brightness dim, so I made myself look away.

All around us the water swirled silently as one by one the islands of the whales' backs slipped under the surface. But one shape began to rise and rise and rise alongside the boat, as if we were in an elevator going down. More and more of the moon-washed sky was blotted out by this living wall lifting out of the sea.

"Yo!" Peter said softly, and nobody told him to shut up.

The giant rolled slowly past our boat in a curve like the curve of a whole planet's horizon, turning back downward toward the deeps: a salute, a farewell.

My throat closed up and my eyes swam.

I had one clear thought out of total left field, or maybe out of some of the memories that Joel had roused up: if only my mom was here—she would finally understand what it was about magic that dazzled! I wished she could see this, because it belonged to her, too, by family right.

Twenty feet away over the empty water, a lone dolphin leaped and did what trained dolphins do in shows. With a whiplash movement of its whole body, it threw me something it had been holding in its mouth.

I grabbed my silver pencil out of the air, the token of my silver wish. The slim wet cylinder burned like ice in my palm. A cool flood of knowing rushed up my arm and through my mind.

I had wished blindness on my mother, and that had blinded me as well. All wishes that try to force other people turn back force on the wisher.

Now, with the dolphin's help, I had canceled the wish that bound my mother—and my own mind cleared. I could "read" this final message that the sea-folk had charged my pencil with as clearly as if the dolphin had delivered a telegram. The pencil was, after all, an instrument of communication.

"Bosanka," I said. "They ask that since you choose to be

hand-folk, like us, you try to use your hands only for helping and healing. They hope you'll teach us to do that, too, for their sakes and our sakes and the sake of everything living on this world."

"Shut up!" she screamed at me. "Shut up, shut up!" Her face was twisted with fury and tears streamed from her swollen, baleful eyes.

Facing that mask of hate, I saw how hopeless the sea-people's wish was. I saw Bosanka's appalling future as an exile living as one of the clumsy, technological hand-folk she despised.

She would become a bitter, miserable, destructive person, cut off from everyone else by her own choice, reaching deeper and deeper into the meanest, angriest, most hurtful parts of herself. She would struggle to keep at any cost the raggedy remnants of the power she remembered having. That old life on a lost and ruined planet would grow more glorious with time, making the present uglier and more repulsive by contrast.

She would become what my mother had always feared becoming, and what maybe I could have become without Mom, or Gran, Paavo, Joel, or the whole Comet Committee for that matter: hateful, cold, hoarding the warped ruins of half-remembered powers—a wicked witch.

I thought of my Gran, the most unwicked witch there ever was, and how one time I saw her hold out her hand to the evil sorceress Ushah in a last attempt to win her away from black magic. Great young talent gone bad and lost, Gran had said later, mourning her enemy. "Sister," Gran had appealed to her. "Daughter, mother, friend."

Well, I wasn't Gran and I couldn't go that far. But I had to do something, because Bosanka's future was unbearable to contemplate.

Even she deserved better.

"Hey, Bosanka,' I said. "It's not the end of the world. I won't leave you twisting in the wind. I'm just a talented lowborn, but I am your student host."

And I put out my hand toward her, but it stopped in midreach, shaking, while a whispery voice quavered in my mind where nobody could hear it but me, "Fine, very generous, but it's the people close to her who'll get to bear the brunt of her grief, her anger, her resentment—and whatever powers she has left. She could destroy you, like a drowning person pulling her rescuer under!

"Sure, Gran offered Horrible Ushah her hand—and remember what happened! Ushah tried to kill her! And besides that, who are you, anyway? You are not your Gran!"

For a second, I thought I had been turned to stone by fear, of what I'd already done and what I was about to do.

But I knew that voice now. Fear, go away, I thought, as fiercely as I could. No, I'm not Gran. I'm Valentine Marsh, and I will do this!

Suppressing a shudder of pure panic, I reached toward Bosanka, trying not to think of what I would or could do if she tried, literally, to drag me over the side of the boat and drown me in vengeful fury.

What she did was go stiff as a board and clamp her eyes shut, but she let me close my fingers around her icy, shaking hand.

Somebody took my other hand—Lennie, that was his chunky mitt. It would be him, I thought, going all sloppy inside with gratitude and relief; warm hand, warm heart, a real softy.

The others took their cue from him. They shuffled around arranging themselves to link hands. Tamsin reached for Bosanka's other hand, completing the circuit.

I saw a faint golden glow on Bosanka's wet face—was the sun coming up?

I thought of the round-cheeked Sun card in Gran's tarot deck—the card that Gran said stood for the heart's desire. We all knew the desire of Bosanka's heart. She had come a long, cold, lonesome way for it, but she would never have it now.

We all knew it, and she saw that we did, and I think that was as hard on her pride as anything.

I tried to make it easier. "I know we're not your people, but we'll do what we can, okay?"

She threw back her matted hair with that gesture I had always thought of as contemptuous. She looked me in the eyes and I believe she read my mind, read her future there, and understood it. A great sobbing breath whooshed out of her.

Then in a low, painful tone she said, "No, you are not. I have done a mistake. Balentena, will you make the light you made on New Year's? Maybe they come back for me. Will you show me to my people?"

Well, we'd come this far, hadn't we? I was willing—but what about Peter and Mimi, who had torn around the park as a couple of deer, and the rest of the committee, forced to the lake by Bosanka's power lines and hunted almost to death?

I said, "You've got the whole Comet Committee here, just as you wanted. Ask them all."

Bosanka resolutely raised her head to face them. "Committee, will you show me to my people?"

There was an awkward silence.

Then Tamsin said irritably, "Well, why didn't you just ask like that in the first place?"

And Peter laughed nervously. And then by God we made a comet.

The boat filled with light that seemed to shine from inside the crooked circle enclosed in our arms and linked hands. A weird, giggly tingling made me feel weightless and insubstantial, as if I were part of one of those skydiving teams, holding hands and falling together.

But we fell upward, toward the sky.

We were brighter than the moon, brighter than the sun. There was nothing anywhere that shone like us as we fell without moving, all the motion existing within us.

Bosanka sat taller, stretching, shimmering with light caught from us. Her hand squirmed and changed in mine. With a tremendous muscular twist she pulled free and leaped up and outward, tearing out of our circle with a painless parting of pure energy.

The rushing in my ears became a tidal roar that was as much light as sound. The brilliance we had been holding among us streamed after Bosanka as she arced through the air backward over the stern of the boat. Her joined legs and feet, now dolphin flukes, hit the water a terrific wallop, dousing me in a freezing drench.

While I still had my eyes squeezed shut and was gasping for breath, I heard my mom's voice. "Valentine? You'd better come with me now. We have to go."

18

The Golden Thread

I opened my eyes. I was sitting half-frozen in the bottom of a rowboat grounded on the littered shore of the rowboat lake, right by the little wooden pavilion. The sawhorses with their Danger signs made shadows that glimmered on the ice under a black, cold, moonlit sky.

"The hospital called," Mom said. She was standing in the pavilion dressed as she had been when she'd left for the day: gleaming silk blouse tucked into her good black pants, with her camel coat hanging open. Her hair spilled in a tangle over her collar.

"They called me out of the writers' conference," she said. "I've been with your Gran since noon. We have to get back there."

Nobody else was in the rowboat except Joel. He crouched in the bow, hugging a bulky object that had to be the violin, inside its battered case again.

"Where'd everybody go?" I asked him. My lips tasted o͏͏ salt, my clothes were still damp, and I was beginning t͏o shiver.

Joel shrugged. "People came for them," he said in a͏ carefully neutral tone. "Like your mom, here, for you."

But nobody had come for him. I gathered myself up t͏o climb out of the tilted boat, stumbling over the oars tha͏t were lying in the bottom. "You'd better come with us, then͏. Mom, can Joel come with us?"

"Yes," she said. I couldn't see her face too well, whic͏h was okay. For the moment, I really wasn't up to explainin͏g why I was in a rowboat with Joel in the middle of the night͏. Or whatever else the lifting of my silver wish had let he͏r understand.

"That's okay," Joel said remotely. "You go ahead wit͏h your mom."

He meant that he wanted to sit there alone until h͏e froze to death or until some one came for him, too. I kne͏w who he waited for, and I didn't think the chances wer͏e very good. "Joel," I said, "come with me to see my Gran͏. Please."

After a minute he came, trudging along behind us throug͏h the nighttime park until we reached the cab Mom had lef͏t waiting outside on Central Park West. We all piled in.

I was too tired to talk. Nobody else said anythin͏g either, thank goodness. At the hospital we went to Gran's͏ room, and Mom sat down with a sigh beside the bed.

"She was awake for a few minutes this morning," Mom said͏, "and then her vital signs started dropping. So they called me.͏"

Gran was not awake now.

"I'm starved, Mom," I said, keeping my voice down͏. "I've got to go find something to eat."

"Bring me something, too," she said, handing me som͏e change from her coat pocket. Mom looked so worn out tha͏t

186

it was harder to look at her than to look at Gran. To my shame, I couldn't wait to get out of there.

Joel put the violin case across the arms of the other chair in the room, and he and I walked down the hallway. The nurse at the station told us there was a candy machine near the water fountain, and we went around the corner she had pointed out. I stopped Joel and stared. "Joel," I said. "That's my Gran. Do you see her?"

"By the fountain?" he said. "Checking out the candy machine?" He saw her.

She looked small and shapeless in a blouse and skirt, summer clothes. The straps of her beige sandals stretched around the bunions on her feet.

"It's all stale," she advised me. "And no shortcake, of course. I'd skip it if I were you, lovie." She sat down on the beat-up brown couch between the candy and the soda machines and smiled at me, patting the cushion next to her.

"Come along, Val," she said, "we need to talk. Congratulations are due—you've done very well indeed, you and your friends. It could have gone so badly that I hate to think of it. But your instincts are good. You'll do."

"Joel," I whispered. "Come on!"

He shook his head violently and stood rooted like a tree, so I walked over alone to sit with my Gran. She radiated a faint warmth, but I noticed that where she sat, the grubby seat cushion didn't sink and crease as if under a solid weight.

I was afraid she would vanish before I could get to ask her all the things I wanted to ask, so I started right in. "Gran, is Bosanka really gone?"

Gran nodded. "Gone to her own, with your good help."

"Well, I hope her people have a better time with their highborn princess than we did," I said. "She was a royal pain, if you ask me."

"She got left behind, remember," Gran said, "and all

that they learned from the death of their world she's missed, you see. She's got a lot of catching up, a lot of maturing to do, now that she's found her own again. They'll help her. They love her, the more so because of what they put her through—for the good of all of them and all of us, mind, but still, there's a great deal owed!

"Of course, that's what a highborn was born for, among them as they used to be—and from her earliest years, she consented to be tested. And what a test! Hers was to be not just any spirit journey, but a special one, a great one, as indeed it was."

I could still hear the echoes of the sea-creatures' voices clicking and whooping in my thoughts, and the mimicry of Joel's violin. "She heard the fiddle that first time Joel played it because it sounded like whales' voices, right?"

"Oh yes, it played their calls," Gran said. "Not that you or Joel or even Lennie would have recognized them. You're used to those sounds as they come out on recording equipment designed for human ears, or wind instruments imitating the sea speech.

"The cetaceans don't actually sing, though, not with their breath. It's something to do with vibrating the bones and oils in their bodies; more like the purring of a cat, really, which is done with the large blood vessels in the chest. At any rate, the violin played her people's calls to her because those calls were stored in it."

"Oh," I said, looking over at Joel. "Then Paavo knew about Bosanka?"

Gran sighed. "We've all known for ages, lovie. The question was what, if anything, to do about her. Paavo was thinking of playing those calls for her when he got finished with your kraken, if he could get the agreement of the sea-people of course. It was all an epic of theirs, remember.

But it was so very hard on her! And he never had the opportunity to try to help."

"You hear that, Joel?" I called.

Gran said, "Softly, lovie. He's listening."

"But how come Bosanka saw our comet on New Year's Eve?" I said. "That was ours, not Paavo's or anybody else's. I was thinking about you, not some royal savage from space! The other people there had stuff of their own in mind. Nobody was trying to get Bosanka's attention."

Gran folded her arthritic fingers in her lap. "Were you happy at the time?"

"With you in here, so sick? Of course not!"

She nodded gravely. "Your own feelings weren't the only ones wrapped up in that spirit light, Valentine. There was a committee. The quality of what you made that night was shaped by the mood of each of you, and in every case the mood was one of anxiety or loss. Well, Bosanka, rattling around a strange world and scared to death that she'd never find her people, was perfectly attuned to all that, and drawn by it."

I said, "She may have been lost and everything, but boy, was she *mean.*"

Gran patted absently at her hair. "She was scared. That's when people are most inclined to do others damage. Don't you agree?"

In view of recent experience—out of fear I had been ready to try to zap Bosanka, remember—I could hardly disagree.

"Besides," Gran added, "'she was so disoriented, Val, that she had very uncertain control of her remaining powers. Which added to her fear, of course, and that made her meaner. She was as used to having magical control as you kids are to turning on light with an electric switch."

"She did deer pretty well," I said.

"Deer was all she could manage, here, and the reality of

189

her home as it is now kept breaking through into her hunting spell besides. Dreadful for you, but not reassuring for her, either, believe me.

"And then of course your committee hadn't much understanding or control of their own powers, either. It's all been quite chaotic. Rather touch-and-go, in fact. The sea-folk were very worried. But I never despaired of you."

Through the faded blue of her eyes I could see light shining, light from behind Gran. Through her whole face, actually, and through her hand when she lifted it to dab at her hair. I tore my thoughts away from this translucence because it scared me, and I didn't want to be distracted right now from what I knew was a pretty important little chat we were having here; for both of us.

But that wasn't a thought I wanted to follow far, either.

No point in asking whether she or anybody from Sorcery Hall would have helped out if we hadn't been able to handle Bosanka ourselves. In magic, as I had reason to know, you play for keeps and you don't count on a rescue by the cavalry.

It looked as if there were a lot of things I just didn't have to ask about anymore. I knew enough to figure out the answers myself.

Which left me with the main question, the one I didn't want to deal with, after all.

I gritted my teeth and I said, "The hospital people think you're dying, Gran."

"Oh, I am," she said.

I couldn't accept this, I wouldn't! Quickly I changed the subject, before I burst into tears. I said angrily, "How come everybody else got met when we came back except Joel? Why didn't anybody come for him?"

"Some one is coming," Gran said. "Don't you see him?"

Then I did see him, strolling toward us from the dead end of the short corridor and dressed in the soft, faded

190

rduroy that I remembered: Paavo Latvela, wizard, musi-
n, warrior, friend.

"Oh," I breathed. "But why is he last, Gran? He should
ve come first!"

"He had the longest way to come, lovie," Gran said,
ning out from the couch to wave at him.

As Paavo passed him, Joel stood with his mouth open
e a boy struck by lightning.

Gran suddenly had her old embroidered handbag in her
and was looking through it for something, which some-
w counted as much as if she had walked away and left
avo and me alone by the candy machine, to talk in private.

I couldn't seem to focus on the details of Paavo's ap-
arance. He was set off by a glare in the lighting, so that he
immered and shifted as I looked at him.

The voice, though, was unmistakable, rough and warm:
good going, Valentine. I won a couple of bets on you."

"Oh, any old time, think nothing of it!" I caroled. I was
led with drunken joy. "But, Paavo, what did I do, exactly?"

"What you think?" Paavo said. He leaned, approxi-
ately, on the side of the candy machine and waited for me
reply, as if he was perfectly ready to change his opinion
meet my answer. He wasn't holding a cigarette, but smoke
rled out of his mouth when he spoke—the memory of that
d habit.

"Well," I said, "I guess I helped the Comet Committee
work some good magic."

"Yah, for a start," he said.

"Oh, no," I said, feeling a jab of dismay as whole
orizons of frustration and annoyance opened ahead of me.
aavo, that doesn't mean I'm stuck with them forever, does
? The whole committee? Even Mimi and Peter, for God's
ke?"

"Ah, Val," he said, blowing more smoke, like a dragon,

not a smoker. "Everybody needs company, a little, anyw
How do you want it, this business of talent? Only for y
only your family? Sha. You want to be lonesome like th
Believe me, it's bad for you."

"Well, now that you mention it," I admitted reluctant
"it sure wasn't good for Bosanka, was it?"

Paavo shook his head. "That poor kid," he said.
meant to try something for her, but—" He shrugged. "Y
don't want to let people fall by the wayside. Thanks
helping out, Valentine. I don't think I could have done
good myself."

It made me cry a little when he said this to me, the w
the winner cries when the Olympic medal is hung arou
her neck and the band plays her national anthem.

Paavo murmured something else that I couldn't catc
something that I felt like a warm touch on my cheek.

"What?" I whispered, leaning forward to try to he
better, see better.

He rippled and almost turned into something else rig
there in front of me. My throat closed up. I was afraid to t
to touch him back. I croaked, "Paavo, are you really here?"

"Here, but not so much Paavo anymore," he said, smoot
ing both big hands down to his waist as if literally pressi
his body back into its Paavo shape. Sorcery Hall games a
played for real, and this wasn't Paavo as he had been,
knew that. This wasn't Paavo in any form I was going to g
to keep around, either.

He didn't give me time to get hysterical over having
let him go a second time.

"Still looks okay, though, right?" he said. "Good.
better go talk with that boy a little, while I can. Sar
Elizabeth, I'll wait for you after, long as I can, yah?"

Gran, dabbing at her hair with a little pink plastic com

odded. "I'll try to be quick," she said, and my heart gave a
ttle hop of alarm.

Paavo turned toward Joel, who backed up a step and
hen stood there, rocking slightly, with this expression of
opeless longing that made me want to cry.

Paavo walked over and reached out to put his hand on
he back of Joel's neck, shaking him a little while he talked
o him. The two of them strolled up and down the hall.

"Where's he going, Gran?" I said squeakily.

"Oh, on, lovie," Gran said. "And so must I. You'll let us
o, won't you? Fussing can detain us a long time, you know.
ut we have our own travels to take up, while you and Joel
nd the others move on in your studies."

I made a grab for her arm, but my hand passed through
omething like warm sunlight. She was up and wavering
lightly in front of me, the way Paavo had wavered.

You lose, I thought; you lose them both.

"Gran, what happened?" I begged. "What did I do
vrong?"

"Why, nothing," she said. "You did most of it right. I'm
o pleased; we've put an application through admissions for
ou. Your work with Bosanka has been found acceptable as
n entrance examination."

"Entrance to what?" I said, getting up to follow her
vhere she drifted, shining faintly, ahead of me.

"To Sorcery Hall, of course," she said. "Bosanka passed
her great test, and you and your friends have passed yours.
You've all passed with flying colors. The Comet Committee
nakes a fine entering class."

I couldn't see her anymore, only a line of light swooping
lown the middle of the hallway, back toward her room. That
ine filled my whole sight, dazzling me so that I couldn't see
oel or Paavo or the nursing station or anything.

So I followed the line, like a blind person feeling he way along a rope. I could actually put my hands on it. Th guideline was warm to the touch.

My shin collided with something, and by looking to th side of the line of light, I saw that I had arrived at the edge Gran's bed. I stood holding a loop in a thread of light tha seemed to come from the center of Gran's still form. Th main length of the line curved away upward into a hug darkness where the ceiling should be.

Gran lay on her back like a doll of dry, yellow wax. Bu the real Gran hovered someplace past sight, tethered to wha was left on the bed by this cord of light. The machine around the plastic oxygen tent over Gran continued to mak their breathing and sighing noises, as if nothing was different

I let go of the golden loop I was holding, and all th length of it that I could see rippled and then slowly resettle itself, floating upward into the dark.

Mom was watching me. Her eyes looked puffy. I won dered how much she could see; everything, I suspected.

"Val," she said, barely in a whisper. "Oh, honey, yo look so *tired*."

I didn't answer. I think I was actually too tired to talk.

My mom is a lot shorter than I am, but she didn't loo it then. There was something tall and firm about the way sh sat in that ugly hospital chair. She showed no sign of fear not even when she turned her head to look up at the line o light, toward where it disappeared into what looked like th deepest place in deep, deep space.

Which was where Gran wanted to go, with Paavo. only she was let free to go.

I ached to help, but at the same time I knew my hand would sooner fly up and throttle me than do what Gra needed done. She'd told me often about how long her ow mother and grandmother had lived, back in Scotland. He forebears were physically little but "tough as old boots," she'd said.

Too tough, now.

"Mom," I said. "I can't do this."

She got up. "You don't have to," she said. "My daughter didn't save me from a wicked wizard for nothing."

She reached up for the line of light above Gran's body and she drew a floaty curve of it down to her own chest level. She bent down to kiss Gran's cheek. Then she parted the thread of light with the lightest, most delicate tug, and she opened both hands and let go.

We watched with streaming eyes as the bright thread curled quickly away and disappeared.

I heard my mother say softly, " 'Bye, Mom."

Then she and the bed and the oxygen tent and all rushed away from me. I toppled like a tree, thinking, Aha, fainting from hunger—you should have had a candy bar while you had the chance.

19

The Hands of Wechsler II

Gran—the part of her that had been lying there living off the support machines—lingered for nearly two more days. Mom and I knew that she was gone long before that. We took our turns at the side of the hospital bed until the doctor was satisfied that what *she* thought was Gran had died.

The members of the Comet Committee came to the memorial service, though most of them had never met Gran. We talked afterward, in the little graveyard attached to the church. It turns out that each of us went somewhere with somebody important to us that night, though nobody went into a lot of detail about it, which seemed to be okay all around.

Anyway, there was good news: Lennie's ear infection had completely cleared up and he was going to Hawaii with his parents on the dolphin project, with special leave from school. He said he had mixed feelings, actually, but I think he was just worried that while he's away, Joel and I are going to get, well, closer.

I told him to relax, nobody was making life decisions here.

"How do you know?" he said, carefully not looking at me. "Looks like a good place for it." He cocked his head at the nearest mossy, tilted stone. The only part of the inscription that hadn't been worn away were the words "Beloved husband."

Corny, but nice.

Our good-byes were a little awkward (what isn't these days? I can't wait to get *older*). I keep hoping that while Lennie's away he'll grow a few inches so he's my height or over.

It's a stupid prejudice, to favor boys who are taller than I am, but I can't shake it. I have not become perfect, I notice. Darn.

Lennie sent me a postcard with a picture of a dolphin on it a week after he got to Hawaii. He sure knows how to make me miss him.

On the postcard he wrote that he feels like he knows all this stuff about cetaceans that nobody else knows, but there's no way to tell it without becoming very unpopular. Scientists are not big on visionary experiences, which is a neat way to put it. So he keeps his mouth shut and helps teach dolphins to do goofy things like carry plastic rings and squares around on their noses.

I guess the maddening part is to know that they're fully sapient beings but not to be able to figure out how to prove it. None of us still have our understanding of the sea-speech from that night, though sometimes Mimi says she almost remembers. But with Mimi, who knows? She reads books about primitive religion and shamanism, but if you ask her a serious question—about what it's like to be a deer, say—she says she doesn't know what you're talking about. She's probably still a ditz, though it's hard to tell.

My mom, who never wanted anything to do with the family talent let alone Sorcery Hall, has figured out her own way to deal with what happened.

"I had a very odd dream," she said to me while we were going through some of Gran's things, picking out stuff for donations and so on. She started describing that night at the lake and the hospital.

"It wasn't a dream," I said. "You know that, Mom."

"Sweetheart," she said, shoving a stack of hatboxes into my arms, "when it comes to this business, you're going to have to go your way, and let me go mine. I did what I could, but I'm the same person I was, and that person does not attend magic school."

And she gave me a look, sort of distressed but determined, that meant this was what she'd intended to say when she brought the subject up: that she's pretty well given up on trying to keep me clear of magic, but that I should count her out.

I can't accept this. I mean, what happened that night was incredible, and I can't stand to see my mom shut herself away from it all. She's a good person, she deserves something special.

Of course, she thinks she has it: Manley has asked Mom to marry him. She could do a lot worse (she almost did, once), and I know, though it really bugs me, that my mother was not designed to live alone.

Barb said, "You got nothing to complain about. At least your mom stays out of your face. Mine is always after me. My clothes are funny, my table manners are crummy, my friends are scuzzy—well, some of my friends, anyway. She thinks you're all right, Valentine. She should know what you've gotten me into!"

"Oh, come on," I said, "how's it different from the juju man your aunt in Barbados knows?"

Barb rolled her eyes heavenward. "My aunt and my mother don't talk about that kind of thing, Valentine. My mother thinks it's extremely racially retro to give any kind of recognition to spook-stuff, as she calls it to avoid using words like 'voodoo.' I can't even show her these pictures."

She had called me over to see what had come out of the Leica, seawater and all. Something had preserved the camera and the film, and the images were of things we had seen with our own eyes that night in the boat—leaping forms curved above shifting waves, the huge bulk of the monster whale rising hazily against the grainy moonlit sky, glimpses of our faces big-eyed and openmouthed or smiling crazily—pictures there hadn't been enough light to take, impossible pictures.

"What are you going to do with them?" I asked.

"Keep them," she said. "I'll just keep them."

We didn't have to say any silly things about not flashing them around to people who wouldn't understand what they were.

I glanced over the whole lot of pictures again. "Funny, there isn't a single picture of Bosanka here."

"I wouldn't keep one if there was," Barb said. "Good-bye and good riddance."

I laughed. "Well, I wasn't exactly thrilled when I figured out that we were just, ah, secondary characters in her heroic quest," I said. "But what the heck, I'm learning to appreciate it."

"Appreciate all you like, Valentine," Barb said. "Are you thinking about writing about it, like it really was a story? If you do, do me a favor. Leave me out of it."

"But you were part of it," I objected. "Even if you did have to put aside some pretty strong feelings, when it came down to it."

"Some feelings don't get put aside."

"Hey, come on," I said. "Did you or did you not help us do that second comet to get Bosanka back to her people?"

She just looked at me.

"Barb," I said. "You did, or we wouldn't have been able to do it!"

She said, "There were seven people in the original Comet Committee. Lennie's right, seven is a special number. With Bosanka herself in the circle, there would have been eight. Joel handed me the violin. I took it so his hands would be free. Joel was your seventh."

She sat on the corner of her dresser and bonked her heel against the bottom drawer, making a hollow rhythm. Her expression dared me to pursue this. So naturally I did.

"If Joel hadn't been there, you wouldn't have pitched in and joined us?"

"Are you kidding? I wasn't about to give that honky creep anything but a kick in her big, square butt." Bump, bump, very ominous.

"So you think we did the wrong thing," I challenged, "helping her?"

"No," Barb said grudgingly. "I know blackness from darkness even if she couldn't tell the difference. You're right, she was all set to get real dark, real bad, meaning wicked. More wicked than she already was, which wouldn't have been good for anybody who had to be around her. So it's better that you all helped her go dolphin."

"But," I said. My calves were cramped from sitting cross-legged so I unfolded my legs, being careful not to mess up the prints laid out all over the bedspread.

Barb shrugged. "But, I wasn't about to join in."

"Okay," I said, "I understand—"

"You don't," she shot back. "You can try, but you don't."

So there was that old no-man's-land that we sometimes found between us, or was it no-friend's-land? I tried to get over it gently. "Heck, true-blue people don't worry about stuff like that."

She let me listen to how lame that was for a minute, which I could clearly hear even over the Skipping Stone Face record she had playing in the background plus the banging of her heel (mad, mad, mad). Then she said, "You mean if I was true blue, I'd have just followed along when you asked me to? Listen, you go ahead and be the Lone Ranger if you want, Valentine, but I am no Tonto!"

"You're telling me," I said. "Tonto means stupid, and you got better marks than I did in the PSATs, so there's no argument there, okay? And if I ever do write this story, I'll put you in saying exactly what you just told me, okay?"

"Okay," she said dangerously. "All right, then. Long as we got this very, very clear." Thump, thump, but not so hard. Our friendship was still solid, and she was not going to give herself a bone bruise and not be able to play basketball next week.

She hopped down from the dresser and came over to study the prints again. "I think this one belongs before this one, don't you? So how am I going to tell Rodney about my PSAT score? He thinks those tests are all fixed in favor of white kids."

"They are fixed," I said, "in favor of mechanical brains, but some of us just manage to transcend these stupid categories so that our natural brilliance shines through."

"Your marks weren't so bad," she said. "Anyhow, writers don't have to be brilliant. Look at what gets published! And my mom reads it *all*."

"Barb," I said, "can I have one of these? I'd like to hang it up in my room."

The picture of the Big One, which you wouldn't even be able to identify as a whale if you hadn't been there, kept drawing my eye. I could almost taste the salt on my mouth and feel the vibration of sea-voices in the air.

"Sure, I'll make you a print," Barb said, glancing at it. "Nice, isn't it?" She selected another one. "I was thinking of making one of these for Lennie."

"But it makes me look like a jerk!" I said.

"Hey, let's see what Lennie says, all right? And maybe this one, for Joel." She pointed at a print of a silhouette of a thin person playing the violin.

We both studied the picture.

Barb said very casually, "So what do you hear from Joel, anyhow?"

There may be trouble ahead.

But I'd rather have trouble and have my best friend than not have my best friend; and Joel is trouble with or without Barb's interest in him. That's just how he is.

I went to a concert with him last weekend. A friend from his school played the piano at Carnegie Recital Hall. Afterward Joel left his friend to her breathless relatives and took me to the Russian Tea Room, where we had delicious little pancakes served by a snooty waiter in a silk shirt.

A lady wearing a fur jacket stopped by just as we were served coffee. She hovered, excusing herself at length for banging Joel's shoulder in passing, gushing and smiling all over him and asking if she hadn't seen him playing a recital recently in Boston.

He admitted that she might have, and she invited him to her table—oh, me too, of course.

"Thank you," Joel said, before I could think of an appropriately devastating response. "I really appreciate the invitation, but I'm afraid my fiancée here breaks out in weeping pustules when she has to sit with people she doesn't know."

The lady bared her teeth, murmured graciously, and swooped away trilling at people she either knew or pretended to know at another table.

I said, "Jeez, Joel. Why not just 'no thanks'?"

He flashed me a wicked grin. "You mean you won't be my fiancée when I need one around?"

"I mean," I said, "that you are definitely not a very nice person sometimes. Lennie is a lot nicer person than you are, basically."

He reared back, affronted. "I'm glad you appreciate the sainted Lennie," he said, then hunched over his water glass and muttered contritely down at it, "Hell, you're right. I have my moments, but I do have my—other moments, too. The point is, even if I did manage to be a nice person all the time, what chance would I have against the sainted Lennie, to whom it comes naturally?"

"If you want a chance, work on it a little," I said. "Lennie's just a person, and who knows who he's busy swimming with down there in Hawaii, anyway? Lots of girls, if Hawaiian girls have any sense. You don't have to measure up to Mother Teresa, you know. A little dependable decency and good manners would do fine."

Instead of laughing, he twirled his glass slowly, staring morosely at the circles the base made on the tablecloth.

"Hey, don't go all broody on me," I said. "Did you play a recital in Boston, like Mrs. La Fur just said?"

He nodded.

"Without letting me know?" I was hurt.

"I was afraid it might be bad," he said in a low voice. "I hardly told anybody."

Another guy in a silk shirt wandered by playing gypsy

music on a violin. Joel rolled his eyes but did not perform any outrages. He was Being Good.

"So how was it?" I said. "Your recital?"

"Not too bad." His eyes lit with pleasure. "It went pretty well, actually."

"You mean your hands are better?" I said eagerly.

"My hands are fine." No more grin. "I think Paavo did it, and you know what? I'm not sure it was worth it." He meant, I think, having his hands cured at the cost of Paavo being really, finally gone.

This was not something I thought we should talk about in the Russian Tea Room or possibly anywhere else for an unforeseeable number of years. I had to make a heroic effort to keep from getting all weepy about Paavo and Gran. Our losses had not been light.

Joel read my expression. He looked shiny-eyed himself.

"Sorry," he muttered, and he sailed right on to something else. "So how are they taking it at school? The Disappearing Foreign Student, I mean."

"Handkerchief, please," I said. He passed his over. I blew my nose. "Mrs. Denby is utterly baffled, and I haven't been exactly helpful, but what can I tell her? She keeps looking at me as if I have personally contributed to the deteriorating image of the Thomas Jefferson School, where Beth Stowers got pregnant and Bosanka Lonat not only disappeared but never lived at the address in the records or knew any of the people whose names she gave them at the office."

"So you're under suspicion?" Joel said. "Oh-oh."

I shrugged. "What can they do to me? There's no corpus delicti, and if there was they wouldn't recognize it."

He tied knots in his napkin to make it look like a rabbit. "She should have been turned into a killer whale at least," he said. "A dolphin—it's too playful, you know? Too popular. There is no justice."

"Well, Joel, you already knew that," I said. I sipped my coffee and wished, not for the first time, that I could get to like the taste. The whipped cream on top was great.

Joel made *Twilight Zone* deetle-deetle noises, turned the napkin-rabbit, and lo, it was actually a whale: the ears had become upraised flukes. "Ta-da!" he said grandly. "My alternative career in magic, demonstrated before your very eyes."

"Not bad," I said.

"Not bad, not great," he said, giving his handiwork a critical look. "Not nothing, when you think of what Bosanka might have had up her sleeve. I think she really was ready to take over the world, mainly because she despised us all and couldn't wait to whip us into respectable shape—tyrannical highborns and lots of cowering undercreatures for them to beat up on for fun. Ugh. I wonder what kind of music they had in her world, before they trashed the whole place? Nothing but drums and horns, I'll bet, played aggressively."

"We only knew her worst side," I reminded him, thinking of what Gran had said. "Her scared side, remember?"

"And barely survived it," he countered. "Are you suggesting that we should have gotten to know her *better*?"

"Well, it might have helped," I said stubbornly. "That's what Lennie said, and I think he understood her better than the rest of us did, being a foreigner himself once."

The fiddler was coming back. Joel looked less tolerant than before.

I said, "Wouldn't it be funny if Lennie ran into Bosanka in her new shape someplace down there in the Pacific?"

"Oh, Lennie," Joel said crankily. "So he's not Mother Teresa, Saint Francis of Assisi isn't much better. Come on, let's get out of here before I do something unforgivable to that so-called musician."

We walked on Fifty-seventh Street, arm in arm, in the cold. "Val," Joel said, "I want to bring the violin over and leave it with you. Just until I feel—I don't know, until I know a little more about things. Is that okay?"

He sounded almost shy, and for a second I couldn't answer. I mean, it was as if Barb were to hand over her camera and her whole darkroom setup to me for safekeeping, which may not sound like a lot, but believe me it is. You don't run into that kind of trust from another person every day.

"Any time," I said, and for a few steps there—before the real world pressed back in on us—we weren't walking but doing some kind of effortless cosmic dance in perfect unison and balance.

"Do you have any idea," he said, checking me in time to keep me from colliding with a mad cyclist, "what comes next? When we start in at Sorcery Hall, I mean? Or how, exactly?"

"You know as much as I do, Joel," I said. "Barb and I were talking about that the other day too. She says the unpredictability is exciting, but that's Barb for you."

"She must lead a quiet life," Joel said drily, "to need that kind of excitement. She should be living in the Caribbean back in the seventeenth century or whatever—Bold Barb the Pirate, that would suit her."

"Joel?" I said as we turned down Fifth Avenue. "Do you like Barb?"

"She's your best friend, isn't she? Of course I like her."

"No, do you *really* like her?"

"What I *really* like," he said stiffly, "is not getting into this kind of conversation. Lay off, will you?"

"Touchy, touchy," I said, regressing rapidly (as I said, I was not yet perfect).

We walked with some space between us for a while.

Some night skaters, headphoned, padded, and costumed, came whizzing quietly down Fifth on roller skates, taking the freedom of the wide, smooth pavement down here where the after-dark traffic was practically nil. They spun down the middle of the avenue like a whirlwind of bulky and fantastic ghosts. One very skinny person in a tutu and a bright red wig was a guy in drag, I was sure.

Watching them wreathe away ahead of us, my thoughts flew free of my nervous social preoccupations. I thought instead of the necromancer's phantom ice skaters, and the dust devil of invisibility that Paavo had made so I could go down into the abandoned subway station on Broadway. I remembered his quick sketch of a circle in a cupful of water that had raised a vision, and Bosanka's pebble waves on the paving at the band shell in the park.

Circles of power, sorcerous reels, magical conga lines were everywhere and never-ending, a dance of marvels both dark and light, if you only had eyes to see it.

Joel caught my hand and squeezed it. "Are you thinking what I'm thinking?" he said. The skaters were gone. "Bosanka's lines of pinecones and twigs, for instance?"

"Among other things," I said.

"Val," he said, "I don't know if I would have come to Castle Lake at noon that day if Bosanka's power lines hadn't pulled me there. I might have chickened out, or just stayed away out of—well, I was ticked off with you. I might have gone right back to Boston."

"No way!" I said. "You knew something was brewing. You wouldn't have missed being in the middle of it this time, you told me so yourself, don't you remember? 'Not this time,' you said. I believed you, even if you didn't."

He looked gratifyingly abashed by my penetrating character analysis.

The skaters erupted again from a side street in a hush of

plastic wheels. A black guy in skintights, black and white spiraling in wide swirls down his trunk and legs, swooped past me—breathtaking, no kidding, like a sleek killer whale. They they all poured away again, out of the path of a thin straggle of headlights following the traffic signals downtown.

With an odd hesitance Joel said, "Val, tell me something: how can you be so right so much of the time and still be so—so—I mean, a regular decent person? How do you keep your balance?"

I heard a real question in there, with some kind of real pain behind it which I couldn't answer. I mean, you can get as close as anything to someone else, and the two of you are still not the same person. But you can sure feel with them.

I said, "Who says I keep my balance?"

"You do it a lot better than I do," he said. "I'm really not as nice as Lennie. Listen, you won't just dump me, will you?"

I thought about that. I thought about Lennie, and about Barb, too, not to mention the person Joel played chamber music with when he wasn't in class playing it—Lisa Walker, her name came back to me. Finally I said cautiously, "If you'll try to keep a little space open for me, I'll try to keep some for you."

"I'm not sure I like the sound of that," he said. "But what the hell, it's a deal."

"Then you can start by coming to my birthday party next week," I said. "I'm going to be fifteen."

"Fifteen!" he exclaimed. "Ye gods, I better get moving—you're *catching up*!"

"Girls mature faster," I said, "everybody knows that. I'm actually way ahead of you already."

"Wait a minute," he said. "Next *week*? For God's sake, and you're just telling me *now*? I have two exams to get ready for, and I'm doing a special performance with Lisa and the others that I have to practice for—"

"Hey, this is my party we're talking about," I said, "not your schedule."

"You don't understand," he said, but I interrupted.

"Listen, Joel, just because you have 'those moments' that doesn't mean I have to stand for them! Lighten up, okay? It's just a party, and whether you can come or not, it's not the end of the world." This was not entirely true, of course. I felt myself winding up to be plenty upset if he didn't come.

"Where do you get off suggesting that your party isn't important to me?" he said with offended dignity. "All I'm doing is reviewing the obstacles so I can figure out a way to get to your party even if it kills me and ruins my career."

And so on. We wrangled enjoyably all the way down to Greenwich Village, where we were meeting Barb (and this photographer she'd met) at a coffee house to hang out and hear some music.

As we walked I caught Joel watching me out of the corner of his eye, just as I slyly glanced at him. He is really beautiful, and it's a pity he knows it. It's amazing what you can see in a person when you remember what you trust, instead of letting yourself get distracted by all the hoops people put each other through more out of habit than anything else.

I wonder what Paavo and Gran were like, when they first got together.

I wouldn't be surprised if they argued a *lot*.

ABOUT THE AUTHOR

SUZY MCKEE CHARNAS is a well-known writer of fantasy and science fiction. *The Golden Thread* is a companion novel to *The Bronze King* and *The Silver Glove*, the first two books in the Sorcery Hall Trilogy. Ms. Charnas's other popular titles include *Walk to the End of the World, Motherlines, Dorothea Dreams, The Vampire Tapestry,* and her novella, "The Unicorn Tapestry," which won a Nebula Award in 1980. She lives with her husband in Albuquerque, New Mexico.

☐ **CAUGHT IN THE ACT: ORPHAN TRAIN
QUARTET, BOOK 2** by Joan Lowery Nixon
In the second novel from THE ORPHAN TRAIN
QUARTET, 11-year-old, Mike fears that he will be sent
back to New York City to serve his prison sentence as
a convicted thief. But the German family which has
adopted him seems to be involved in much worse than
stealing—murder! Mike vows to uncover the truth, even
if his own life is in danger.
27912-2 $2.95/$3.50 in Canada

☐ **THE GIRL WHO INVENTED ROMANCE**
by Caroline B. Cooney, author of 'Among Friends'
As she watches her friends and family playing at romance, 16-year-old Kelly Williams has a great idea—
she'll create a board game that sets down the rules of
the romance game. It's easy for Kelly to see how others
should act, but it's much more difficult when it comes to
her own feelings for Will! (A Starfire Hardcover).
05473-2 $13.95/$15.95 in Canada

STARFIRE

Intelligent Fiction For Teens.

☐ **NOW THAT I KNOW** by Norma Klein
28115-1 $2.95/$3.50

☐ **THE SEBASTIAN SISTERS: EVVIE AT SIXTEEN** by Susan Beth Pfeffer
28075-9 $2.95/$3.50
Beginning with EVVIE AT SIXTEEN, this five-book series follows the
lives of the SEBASTIAN SISTERS as each girl turns sweet sixteen! It's
not easy to adjust to a life that's like a roller coaster; thanks to
beloved Dad's wheelings and dealings the Sebastian family is at
times very rich and at times very poor. This is one of the poor
times, and Evvie spends the summer as a companion to her rich
Great-Aunt Grace. Through a summer of intriguing romance and
surprising scandal, Evvie learns that love is stronger than logic
anytime!

☐ **THE SEBASTIAN SISTERS: THEA AT SIXTEEN** by Susan Beth Pfeffer
28195-X $2.95/$3.50

☐ **THE SEBASTIAN SISTERS: CLAIRE AT SIXTEEN** by Susan Beth Pfeffer
28460-6 $2.95/$3.50

☐ **THE SEBASTIAN SISTERS: SYBIL AT SIXTEEN** by Susan Beth Pfeffer
28614-5 $2.95/$3.50

Buy them at your local bookstore or use this handy page for ordering:

Bantam Books, Dept. DA23, 414 East Golf Road, Des Plaines, IL 60016

Please send me the items I have checked above. I am enclosing $_____
(please add $2.00 to cover postage and handling). Send check or money
order, no cash or C.O.D.s please.

Mr/Ms _____

Address _____

City/State_____ Zip_____

DA23–9/90

Please allow four to six weeks for delivery.
Prices and availability subject to change without notice.

STARFIRE®

For Memories That Will Last.

PEOPLE LIKE US
by Barbara Cohen   ☐ 27445-7/$2.95

"Don't Start What You Can't Finish..."
When gorgeous quarterback Geoff Ruggles asks Dinah Adler out, she is ecstatic. But when Dinah decides to invite him to her brother's Bar Mitzvah her family will not allow it, because Geoff is not Jewish. Dinah can't understand how her loving family can suddenly be so unfair and hypocritical. Does Dinah have to choose between her family and her own happiness?

THE YEAR WITHOUT MICHAEL
by Susan Beth Pfeffer   ☐ 27373-6/$2.95

"It Couldn't Happen to Us!"
Bad things aren't supposed to happen to good people. So when 15-year-old Jody Chapman's younger brother Michael disappears, she can't believe it. He wouldn't run away—but then where is he? And how can her family survive the pain of not knowing? This riveting novel explores family ties in times of unexpected crisis.

SUMMER OF MY GERMAN SOLDIER
by Betty Green   ☐ 27247-0/$3.50

Awkward, lonely Patty Bergen was twelve the summer that the World War II German prisoners arrived at the POW camp outside Jenkinsville, Arkansas. Then she meets Anton, a German prisoner. A strong and dangerous friendship develops and changes their lives *forever*.